RHYTHM AND HUES - TWENTY-THREE STORIES OF HARDSHIP AND HOPE

Corey B. Collins

DORRANCE PUBLISHING CO
EST. 1920
PITTSBURGH, PENNSYLVANIA 15238

The contents of this work, including, but not limited to, the accuracy of events, people, and places depicted; opinions expressed; permission to use previously published materials included; and any advice given or actions advocated are solely the responsibility of the author, who assumes all liability for said work and indemnifies the publisher against any claims stemming from publication of the work.

All Rights Reserved
Copyright © 2022 by Corey B. Collins
No part of this book may be reproduced or transmitted, downloaded, distributed, reverse engineered, or stored in or introduced into any information storage and retrieval system, in any form or by any means, including photocopying and recording, whether electronic or mechanical, now known or hereinafter invented without permission in writing from the publisher.

Dorrance Publishing Co
585 Alpha Drive
Pittsburgh, PA 15238
Visit our website at *www.dorrancebookstore.com*

ISBN: 978-1-6386-7008-7
eISBN: 978-1-6386-7957-8

RHYTHM AND HUES - TWENTY-THREE STORIES OF HARDSHIP AND HOPE

CONTENTS

LOSS 6
Sketchy Recollection 7
Hair Today 17
Fathers and Sons 24

PURPOSE 32
With Good Trouble and Justice for All 33
Wonder Women 39
Who You Know 49
The Fork 60
The Worst 67

PRIVILEGE 70
Any Little Extra 71
Self-Evident Truths 79
Small Talk 86

LAUGHS 95
The Case 96
Girls 99
The Chloe Chronicles 101
Tryin' 106

PERSPECTIVE 109
The Cycle 110
Sanguinity With a Side of Silver Fish 117
More Than Enough 120
Two Good Eggs 124

HOPE 131
Greeny's Gamble 132
The Hero, the Healer and Harvey 135
Vestiges 142
A Woman's Worth 146

LOSS

SKETCHY RECOLLECTION

It all began a few months before she turned five. She would draw the oddest pictures— sketches really—of people in distress, then cry immediately after drawing them. And she wouldn't weep lightly. She would burst into the most gut-wrenching sobs I'd ever seen for a child her age, sometimes doubled over at the waist, other times flailing her arms wildly, kind of like the old ladies at the funerals Mama used to take me to when I was a boy. One day she didn't stop crying until she fell asleep, draped across the small desk we put in her room, her arms dangling like little Christmas tree ornaments. I watched her as she slept that day, noticing the restless way her fingers and head twitched every couple of minutes, as if someone were shooting tiny volts of electricity through them.

When she woke up, I would scoop her into my arms and held her close like a father should. I always wondered why she continued to draw those pictures when they caused her so much pain. At times I would try to talk her out of drawing altogether, as did Mother—that's what I started calling my wife after Pru was born—but she would hear nothing of it. She just kept drawing, safeguarding her sketches in the mysterious green box the little old lady gave her at the winter fair. A lot of time has passed since then, but I can remember that day at the fair like it was yesterday.

It was midafternoon on the day Pru turned five years old. Mother and I had just bought her first cotton candy. As soon as we strolled past the booth with the "TABLE OF FORTUNE" sign hovering above it, the little old lady released the palm she was reading, stood up, looked frantically from side to side, grabbed the green box from her shelf and sprang out of the booth. She rolled her head anxiously from right to left, as if she were running out of time. That's when she spotted us—Mother, Pru, and me. She sprinted toward us like an Olympian bounding towards the finish line and stopped right in front of Pru, her shoulders rising and falling quickly with each breath. She knelt down, dodging the sticky glob of sugar protruding from Pru's left hand and placed the green box inside Pru's right hand. Then, she craned her neck towards Mother and me and spoke.

"Listen to this child. She has many important things to say."

Seconds later, the little old lady was gone.

Thinking back, Pru already had begun to speak quite well up to that point, but by no one's definition was she the most talkative child in the world—not in words anyway. Instead, Pru would draw pictures and from that day forward, as soon as she finished, she would fold and house them in the green box given to her by the little old lady. Then, she would hide the box, only taking it out on her birthdays. She would ask Mother and me to take her to a number of different places on each of her birthdays and we would always try to honor her requests.

Wherever we went on her birthdays—and we sometimes took her to several places—without fail she would take that green box with her. I noticed that, every so often, she would remove a drawing and give it to someone, many times to total strangers, tears welling in her eyes as she parted with her drawings. She continued this ritual for a number of years, engaging in what can only be described as rather obsessive behavior, until one year she just stopped. I think it was the day Pru turned ten. On that day, I woke up first, like always, promptly at 6:00 a.m. and made my way downstairs for my morning coffee and smoke.

On most days, after starting the coffee, I would go right outside to collect the morning paper, but on that morning, I lingered in the house a little longer than usual. Once I started the coffee, I meandered toward the pantry to return the remaining coffee filters. As I did so, I heard the faint sound of whimpering, which I first thought to be a dog or cat. The high-pitched, muffled words that were spoken next convinced me I was wrong.

"Too late, I was too late!"

I knew immediately that it was a woman's voice, one that sounded familiar to me. As I approached the front door, the sound grew louder and clearer. I flung open the door and saw Kate Sanford, one of Mother's friends from down the street, standing on the front porch. She wiped tears from her face with her left hand as she grasped and crumpled something in her right hand. Kate and Mother had grown to be pretty close over the years, both of them having daughters around the same age. Like Mother and me, Kate and her husband, Dexter, were one of the only couples of color in town. I am convinced that this fact made the bond between Mother and Kate that much stronger, as I could not help but recall several occasions when I overheard them comparing notes like only two "sisters" could—about things like what ingredients work best to season a pot of collards or what oils were most effective at combating the oftentimes challenging textures of their daughters' hair.

Kelly—that was Kate's daughter—and Pru had grown to be pretty close too, each joining the school speed-skating team the year before; each harboring not-so-secret desires to make the Olympic team someday, especially after watching Vonetta Flowers—the first African-American in history—win a gold medal at the Salt Lake City Winter Games earlier that year.

Noticing Kate's obvious pain, I spoke.

"What's the matter? What happened?"

"Pru, I want to see Pru," a distraught Kate said. She steadied her left hand against the wall, struggling to maintain her balance.

"Well, it's pretty early," I said. "She's still sleep—"
"I need to see her now!" Kate interrupted. "Take me to her! Please!"
Fearing what would happen next if I denied her request, I escorted Kate to Pru's room. By the time we reached her room, there was no need to jostle Pru awake. Kate's ear-piercing wails already had caused Pru to stir. Kate fell to her knees when she reached Pru's bed and extended the hand that housed the wrinkled paper towards Pru.

"I was too late! Why didn't you give this to me sooner than yesterday? Why didn't you just tell me?"

Pru lay in her bed, transfixed, staring at Kate with knowing and apologetic eyes. She fixed her lips as though she wanted to say something but couldn't. I crouched between Kate and Pru, intercepting the wad of paper that still remained in Kate's hand. I unraveled it, smoothing out the edges so I could make out the picture reflected there. By that time Mother had entered Pru's room, undoubtedly awakened by Kate's screams.

"What's going on?" Mother asked.

No one answered Mother. Pru's eyes remained fixed on Kate. Kate continued to weep, swiveling her head toward Mother, her intermittent tears falling from her face like drops from the bathroom faucet I'd been meaning to fix. Meanwhile, my body began to grow numb, shocked by the portrait I continued to study as Kate cried. It was Kate's daughter Kelly suspended beneath a pond of water, her little eyes looking helpless and frightened.

"I found her this morning, floating in the pool," sobbed Kate. "She must have slipped and fallen in. And we were just going to start her swimming lessons at the community center next week. It must have been awful!"

It took several hours for Mother and me to calm Kate that day. I don't believe Pru was able to make eye contact with Kate on that day or ever again, much less talk to her.

From that day forward, Pru stopped drawing altogether. Or so I thought. On the day she turned fifteen, which happened to coincide with the day of the big speed-skating competition, Pru awoke early, no doubt eager to get to the ice-covered pond to practice before everyone else arrived. A good showing that day would have guaranteed a spot for her on the state team. She must have come down the stairs super early that morning because I noticed the light in the kitchen already was on when I came down at six. As I rounded the corner that connected the living room to the kitchen, I found Pru huddled over the kitchen table, scribbling furiously like she was taking a test, anxious to complete all her answers before her time expired. As soon as she noticed I was there, she stopped writing, folded the page, then inserted and sealed it in a big manila envelope. She wrote the name "Alan Parker" on the envelope, handed it to me and hugged me. When she released me, I noticed a tear had formed in her right eye. She forced a smile, extended the envelope toward me, then kissed me on the cheek.

"Please take this to Mr. Parker at 7:30 this morning, Daddy," she said. "Promise me."

The look in Pru's eyes was one I had not seen before. It was a look of fear I knew I could not calm. Instead, I gently stroked her hair and pulled her close.

"I promise," I said.

Pru threw on her overcoat, flung her skates over her left shoulder and bounded out the door. Before she left the house, she spoke.

"I love you, Daddy."

And then she was gone. After she left, I resumed my routine. I made coffee, collected the paper and had my morning smoke, the whole time concerned about what Pru could have left in the envelope for Parker. At 7:00, I was heading out the door on my way to Parker's when I heard Mother yell from the top of the stairs.

"Where are you going?"

"I need to run an errand," I replied. "I'll be back shortly."

"Where's Prudence?" Mother asked. "She's not in her room."

"She's at the pond warming up for the competition," I replied. "It's today, remember?"

"Oh, yes, I remember now. Why she insists in competing in that sport I'll never know. It's so unladylike, but what else is new? Anyway, hurry back because I need you to hang the new family portrait. You know the picture we sat for last week when Prudence actually was in one of her better moods? It arrived yesterday."

"I would love to, dear," I replied, "but, you made me get rid of all my tools, remember?"

"Oh yeah," she giggled. "You don't have them anymore. And I *so* wanted to hang the portrait today. I guess we'll just have to wait. Oh, pooh!"

"Well, I guess I could pick up a hammer over at Parker's," I replied. "I mean, that's where I'm heading now anyway. I'm sure he has some of them in stock."

"Only if you want to, dear," Mother said. "I don't want to make you feel as though you have to do something you really don't want to do."

"It's no problem," I replied. "I'll be back soon."

Then, I left. As I drove toward Parker's, I began to chuckle thinking about the deceptive way Mother always managed to get people to do what she wanted. When I first met her, I was immediately drawn to the syrupy sweet demeanor she displayed for every audience she encountered no matter what the occasion or circumstance. At first, I thought it was just too good to be true, that a person could be so nice all the time. Soon, I realized that the charming disposition she displayed to the world in reality was oftentimes a very effective tool she routinely used to manipulate people to her advantage. Like on the day we had our first date. I took her to the best seafood restaurant in town. As I steered my truck into the restaurant parking lot, she spoke.

"Oh, I didn't know you were taking me to a seafood restaurant. I don't really like seafood."

"I'm sorry, I didn't know," I replied. "We can go somewhere else."

"No," Mother replied. "That's okay. I'm sure I can try to find *something* on the menu I can eat."

"But, why should you have to?" I asked. "Particularly when there are a number of other restaurants—"

"No, no, no," Mother interrupted. "This is perfectly fine, John. You obviously chose this place because you like the food here. I know that lots of people rave about it. I don't want you to change your plan on my account. Let's just go in. I'll be fine."

"Only if you're sure," I said.

"I'm positive," she replied.

And we went inside. As soon as we walked inside the door, I noticed Mother making faces and twitching her nose like something in the air didn't sit well with her.

"Are you sure you're okay?"

"I'm fine," Mother replied. "Let's just get a table."

"Okay," I said.

By that time, the hostess had approached us and proceeded to escort us to a booth. As soon as we folded ourselves into our seats, a plump little woman with ample hips and thick rosy cheeks walked toward us, handing us our menus. She proceeded to take out her order pad to which I could not help but notice was attached a large coupon for McDougal's Hamburgers. Mother glanced at the coupon too, then down at the menu, flipping through its pages as though she were seriously considering the numerous selections displayed there. Then, she spoke to no one in particular.

"Hmmm. I have an appetite for a burger."

She looked up at the waitress and spoke.

"You all don't happen to serve them here, do you?"

"No," replied the waitress. "But, you know, I was just thinking the same thing. Which reminds me, I'm scheduled to take my break in a few minutes so someone else probably will be bringing your food out. I just wanted you to know so you wouldn't be surprised."

Then, she leaned toward Mother and me and whispered.

"Don't tell anyone, but I'm gonna run down the street on my break and use this coupon for two double deluxe burgers at McDougal's."

She slid the coupon from beneath her order pad and showed it to us.

"Oh!" Mother exclaimed. "You've got my mouth watering just thinking about it. McDougal's has the best burgers. They're my personal favorite, you know?"

Then, she sighed and winked at me.

"I guess I can find *something* on this menu."

"Can you give us a few minutes?" I asked.

"No problem," the waitress replied. She looked at Mother with a sympathetic smile, then moved away from the table.

A few minutes later, we noticed the waitress exit the front door of the restaurant, heading down the street to pick up her burgers, we presumed. Soon thereafter, Mother and I finally placed our orders with the waitress's replacement. I ordered the lobster tail. Mother ordered chicken and chips. Just before our order arrived, our first waitress re-entered the restaurant, walked directly towards our table, her right hand tucked inside her overcoat like Napoleon, as though she were on official business. Or hiding something. We would soon discover she was doing both. She approached our table, leaned down toward Mother and spoke.

"This is for you."

She removed her hand from beneath her coat revealing the McDougal's bag and gently placed it on the table in front of Mother.

"I like a gal who can appreciate a good burger," the waitress said.

Then, she turned and headed back toward the kitchen, her hips rising and falling like a seesaw as she strolled away.

"Oh, she didn't have to do that, but it sure was nice of her," Mother said. She glanced at me and winked. I summoned our new waitress and canceled Mother's chicken and chips order.

Over time, Mother's powers of persuasion began to have obvious, noticeable effects on me. From the way I dressed (she hated overalls) to the food I ate (I haven't eaten lobster since the day after Mother's vivid description of the parasites that have a fondness for their shells), Mother always had a way of getting me to do things her way. But, I must say that the most influential change she made on my life was when she persuaded me to get rid of all my tools.

After fifteen years of carpentry and handiwork, shortly after Pru was born, Mother would drop not-so-subtle hints about her feelings on the danger of tools. She would copy articles about children who had suffered horrible accidents, or worse, at the hands of household tools. Then, she would strategically place them in locations where I could not help but see them—like in the garage or on top of the remote control or on the seat of my recliner. Within a week, there wasn't a tool to be found in the house. I got rid of all of them. From that time on, no one would have ever known I had been one of the most successful carpenters in town if I didn't tell them.

Mother's influence seemed to be just as effective with everyone she came in contact with—everyone except Pru, that is. From the time she was a toddler, Pru always displayed an undeniably independent and rebellious spirit, one Mother never could tame no matter how hard she tried. And in the beginning, she did try. Like the time Mother attempted to "cure" Pru of her obsession with tanks, trucks, Army men, and other war toys, items Pru first discovered while playing with little Bobby Tucker at preschool. The announcement came on the very first day Mother found Pru on her bedroom floor after school with little war toys she had borrowed from Bobby spread across the carpet.

"This will stop today," Mother said.

She left the house soon thereafter only to return an hour later with a bag full of dolls. Instead of taking the dolls to Pru's room, Mother began to play with them herself in the family room. She dressed them in the various outfits that came with each one, deciding which little shoes worked best for which particular outfit. Just as Mother began to comb one of the doll's hair, Pru bounded down the stairs, no doubt with intentions of inquiring about the status of her pre-dinner snack. Upon seeing Mother, Pru froze and fixed her eyes on the doll Mother was holding, as Mother maneuvered the doll's head to one side while gently running a brush through her hair. Within seconds, Pru had collected the remaining dolls that surrounded Mother's feet and raced upstairs. As we heard the door to Pru's bedroom shut, Mother turned toward me and winked. I winked back.

Less than an hour later when it was time for dinner, Mother and I climbed the stairs to gather Pru. As we did so, Mother spoke.

"I can hardly wait to see how she's doing with her new friends."

As she opened the door and poked her head inside to announce dinner, Mother's mouth fell open when she surveyed the little plastic heads and limbs spread across Pru's bedroom floor. I must admit that I, too, was a bit taken aback at the scene. Pru had beheaded and de-limbed each doll, placing some heads atop little plastic rifles she had stuck in the carpet and positioned some of the limbs inside the raised hands of little toy soldiers. Mother shook her head, turned around and trudged back down the stairs.

"I can't do anything with her. She's all yours."

At that moment, Pru lifted her head, looked at me and winked. I winked back.

As I continued to drive toward Parker's, I reached inside my overcoat to make sure the manila envelope Pru had given me was still there. It was. Then, I thought about how ironic it was that on the one day I actually needed a hammer, I happened to be heading toward the home of one of the town's most successful hardware men. Many years ago, when he was still a carpenter, Parker had been my biggest competition for business. Now, he almost cornered the hardware market, particularly with the full-service hardware store he had built next to his home.

I knew that picking up a hammer would be no problem that morning as I thought how nice it would be to handle another tool again after all these years. It was precisely 7:30 when I arrived at Parker's. He, like I, was an early riser. He opened the door as I walked up his driveway holding his morning paper (he was heading out to pick it up). As I handed him the newspaper, I also handed him the manila envelope.

"It's from Prudence," I said.

"What is it?" he asked. He grabbed the envelope with one hand and tucked the newspaper underneath his arm with the other. He then broke the seal of the envelope. Inside, he noticed another smaller envelope and a separate folded piece of paper. The smaller envelope had the words "open this first" on it. So, he did. Inside the envelope was a sheet of paper, which read:

Please give Daddy a sledgehammer. Here is the money to pay for it.

"What an odd request," Parker said. "I haven't put them in my store yet, so I'll have to get one from over here."

He walked towards his garage in his overcoat and slippers. He opened the garage door, pulled out a three-foot sledgehammer and handed it to me as soon as I stood in the driveway. He then headed back to the front door. Just then, I remembered the hammer Mother wanted me to get and I asked Parker if he had any in stock. He said he did, but that most of them were at his new store. He did say he had a couple in his home office that had not yet been shelved and asked if I could give him a few minutes while he went to get one. I said yes and waited for him by his front porch.

After what seemed like an eternity (almost twenty minutes), Parker returned with the hammer and handed it to me. I noticed the sticker on the arm of the hammer read $3.25, then tugged at my pockets, realizing my wallet was not there.

"My money's in the truck," I said. "Give me a second."

I headed back to the truck to retrieve my wallet and gave Parker the money when I returned. I shook Parker's hand and turned to head back to the truck when I heard Parker's voice.

"Wait! The second sheet of paper!"

By that time, I was inside the truck looking at Parker through the windshield. As he tore into the manila envelope for a second time and unfolded the second sheet of paper, his face began to turn as white as the coat of paint that covered his house. He dashed toward the truck, reached through the partially opened window and thrust the paper into my hands. I stepped out of the truck and looked at the paper. Tears rolled down my cheeks as the recognition of frightened eyes in the sketch descended upon me. The likeness was uncanny and I could not help but notice that the face depicted on the page seemed to be obstructed in a way. The more I looked at the drawing, the more apparent it became that the eyes peering back at me were trapped behind—or underneath—something. It was as if they, or she, were trapped and could not escape.

Then, it occurred to me. The pond. Instinctively, I jumped back inside my truck and turned the key to start the ignition. As I sped toward the pond, my mind rushed back to the morning I found Kate on our doorstep all those years earlier grasping the tear-stained sketch Pru had drawn of her daughter she had found at the bottom of her swimming pool—the daughter she was unable to save.

I wondered if I would be able to save mine.

At the moment, I asked myself this question, I glanced at my watch. 8:10. How much time did I lose waiting for Parker to bring me the hammer so I could hang the family portrait for Mother? Why didn't I make Parker look at the second piece of paper sooner? How cold was it outside?

As I rounded the bend and craned my head toward the pond, there was no sign of Prudence anywhere. I parked the truck, jumped out and ran toward, then onto, the ice-covered pond, sliding as I moved. Then, I saw them—splashes from a small opening in the distance, an opening that seemed to have been created by one of the few patches of sunlight that had managed to break through the canopy of trees that had cast a massive shadow across most of the pond. I scurried quickly toward the opening in the pond.

When I got there, I looked down and saw the most horrific sight any father could imagine. I saw my daughter's arms flailing beneath the ice as though she were looking for something to hold onto for safety. She was too far away from the opening, so I kneeled down and motioned for her to swim in its direction. Either she did not see me or she did not understand because she remained in the same spot. Frantically, I began to jump up and down on the ice right above her, hoping my body weight would cause the ice to crack open so I could reach her in time. I cursed myself for allowing Mother to convince me to go on that diet a month ago, which had caused me to lose ten pounds. The ice did not crack.

Then, I thought—the sledgehammer! I scampered quickly across the ice back to my truck, threw open the door and found the sledgehammer wedged beneath the passenger seat. I grabbed the sledgehammer and ran back onto the pond. After at least seven falls, I finally arrived at the section of the ice that trapped my daughter. By the time I began to strike the ice with the hammer, Pru had stopped moving, her hands positioned upward, next to her face. Then, I noticed the eyes—the same eyes I had seen earlier that morning before she left the house, the same eyes I had seen in the sketch she gave to Parker—peering directly at me, motionless. I collapsed on the ice and wept for what seemed like an eternity, hoping against hope that I somehow was locked inside a bad dream and that any moment the six o'clock alarm would sound, jolting me awake, allowing me to escape. But, the alarm did not sound, and I already was awake and my daughter was not moving.

As the days, months and years passed, the pain eventually became a little less sharp, like a knife that begins to dull over time. I still hold on to the sketch. I don't know why. Perhaps it's because I want to be reminded of how extreme pain, extreme helplessness feels. Each time I look at the terror-filled eyes in the sketch, I then look at the family portrait I finally garnered the strength to hang a year after Pru's death and I'm reminded of the few happy times in her life—and of her independence. But, in the end, I always find myself thinking about the sadness that seemed to follow her most of her life. What a burden it must have been for her. What was the last thing she said to me when she left the house on that last day? Oh, I remember....
I love you, Daddy!
"I love you too, sweetheart. Rest well, now."

HAIR TODAY

"Look at her, child! She look like she ain't combed her hair in a year!" Sadie clucked. She dipped her head in Doris's direction.

"Girl, you know they say that rich man of hers don't allow her to go to the beauty shop no mo' 'cause he believe 'dem chemicals seep down into her brain and make her get the vapors," Claudine laughed. She proceeded to scan the items of food that crept down the conveyor belt of her "ten items or fewer" express lane.

Doris slowly made her way up the condiment aisle toward the front of the *Pig & Pantry* as Sadie and Claudine spoke. Doris smiled and waved at them as she glanced over at the checkout lanes. She continued to frequent the neighborhood grocery store despite now living twenty miles away, all in an effort to remain close to the community in which she was reared. By all accounts, Doris had "made it" with her successful career in nursing and marriage to her childhood sweetheart Anthony Tucker, the star short stop of the St. Louis Redbirds. Nevertheless, she felt the pull of locations and people who reminded her of simpler times, especially now. Doris's shopping cart lurched and squeaked from the weight of the items protruding from its sides as if it were a lumbering elephant in search of a quiet spot to rest.

Doris, Claudine, and Sadie had been thick as thieves for the greater part of their lives really. Since the time Doris and her mama had moved to the community when Doris was six, Doris, Claudine and Sadie had been integral parts of virtually every significant milestone of each other's lives, especially during their formative years. Doris stared at her friends, certain they were gossiping about her from the looks on their faces. As she continued her advance toward the front of the store, she reminded herself of the many times they'd supported each other in the past—through deaths of grandparents, siblings' transitions from high school to college, not to mention their transitions to womanhood. She contemplated these events as she reflected on the words Claudine and Sadie spewed from their lips like snake's venom. She was convinced they had no idea she could hear their gossiping about her admittedly wretched state. The doctors had said one of the potential side effects of her ailment was the heightening of her senses. So, being privy to a conversation whispered thirty feet away did not surprise Doris.

Though she hated to admit it, Claudine and Sadie were only bringing voice to what she was sure others also observed about her appearance. Truth be told, Doris could not remember the last time she'd actually sat down to give the thick, raven-black, long curly mane she inherited from the Indian branches of her family tree the attention it required. Over the past several weeks, such a luxury had been the least of her worries. As hurtful as the words her friends spoke were, Doris could not fault them so much, as she knew she was the one who had made the conscious decision *not* to let them in on the secrets she had been guarding for the past six months.

Doris deposited the last food item into her shopping cart as it rolled noisily toward the checkout line. She could not even think of playing the friendship card with the number of items in her cart as she eased away from Claudine's express line and steered her cart toward Sadie's.

"Hey, girl!" Sadie exclaimed. She caught the package of chicken wings that tumbled from Doris's cart when it collided with the outer edge of Sadie's checkout counter.

"Hey," Doris laughed. "I'm sorry, girl. As you can see, it's been a minute since I've been up in here. I'm practically buying the whole store out today."

"Well, you can afford it," Sadie replied. She inserted the wings into a plastic bag, then adjusted the faux ponytail she had carefully clipped onto the back of her head hours earlier. She reached for the next item in Doris's cart, as she continued to speak. "I know you probably been real busy with all you must be doin' these days. Me and Claudine was just talkin' about how we ain't seen you in what feel like a year!"

"Uh-huh," Doris replied. "I been kinda busy with work and taking care of some other stuff. And Anthony and Lil A.J. are a handful, as I'm sure you can imagine, girl."

"Yeah, I don't doubt it," Sadie said. "But don't be a stranger, girl. Remember how we used to hang out all the time?" she asked, while gesturing toward Claudine. "Seem like a lifetime ago now, though."

"I know what you mean," Doris replied. "Let me get past this busy patch and we'll get it back on track. I promise."

"We betta," Sadie replied. "You our girl. We go way back. We miss you!"

"Awww. I miss y'all too!" Doris said. She swiped her credit card, while waving to Claudine.

"Call us, girl," Sadie said. She handed a foot-long receipt to Doris.

"I will," Doris lied, as she and her squeaky, oil-deprived shopping cart slowly exited the store.

"She ain't gon' call us," Sadie said to Claudine less than ten seconds after Doris's departure.

"Nah, she ain't," Claudine replied.

* * *

"I sure wish you would do something with yo' hair!" Mama exclaimed before ingesting the last of her pills for the evening. Doris shook her head and adjusted the goose-down pillows on Mama's king-sized bed, positioning them so as to make the perfect receptacle for Mama's head.

Doris and Mama had been on opposite ends of many legendary battles over the years. Doris knew when Mama drew a line in the sand and proclaimed she would be recuperating from her illness in the quiet and comfort of her own home, however, there was no argument to be had. Doris wondered, then, why Mama had chosen tonight of all nights, to engage on an issue Doris viewed as having so little significance.

"Mama, now you know my hair is the last thing I'm worried about right about now," she said.

"Well, if you gon' sit here and try to make my challenge an excuse for you not taking care of yourself, then...."

"Then what, Mama?" Doris asked. "Are you saying I should put my vanity ahead of your care giving?"

"Well, you know what they say," Mama replied. "Look at the state of a woman's hair and that'll tell you about the state of her house."

"Well, I admit it," Doris replied. "My house ain't in order right now."

"Well, mercy," Mama replied. "She done told the truth."

"And guess what, Mama?" Doris said. "I don't care. And you know why?"

"Why?" Mama asked.

"Because I got something more important to attend to right now," Doris said. She massaged Mama's back to ease the pain. "And she sittin' right here."

"Ahhh," Mama moaned. "All right. All right. But that husband and son of yours need to be high up on that list as well. And yo' hair need to be up there too!"

"Mama!" Doris laughed. "What am I gon' do with you?"

"Absolutely nothin'," Mama replied.

"Enough of this crazy talk, lady," Doris said. "Now get some rest."

Doris carefully adjusted the bedspread around Mama's shoulders, then draped the stethoscope she'd used ten minutes earlier to monitor Mama's heart around her neck. She regretted not telling Mama the secret she had been harboring for the past three months, but she knew it was for the best. She inclined her head downward to plant a soft kiss on Mama's cheek. "I love you, Mama."

"I love you too, baby," Mama replied. She closed her eyes.

* * *

"If you keep your hair pinned up like that, babe, it's just fine with me," Anthony said. He adjusted his impeccably tailored suit while standing in front of the full-length mirror in one of four downstairs bathrooms in the couple's three-story mansion, then straightened his tie.

"Why is everybody so concerned about my hair?" Doris replied. She and Anthony had been married for the better part of ten years now, but they had known each other for what seemed like an eternity, having grown up literally a block from each other. Though he was a few years older, Doris and Anthony, like Doris, Claudine, and Sadie had also been present for many of the major events of each other's lives. Doris had witnessed seven-year-old Anthony's first home run in Pee Wee Baseball as she jumped up and down on the sidelines with pom-poms in hand while her already full-length ponytails lightly slapped against her cheeks.

Anthony had been there when an eleven-year-old Doris received the top prize at the tri-county science fair. Doris had been there when a twenty-year-old Anthony was called up to the majors and got placed on the Redbirds roster. Anthony had been there when a twenty-six-year-old Doris received her nursing degree from Johns Hopkins University..

Years ago, Doris tried to ignore Claudine and Sadie's protestations that she and Anthony's union as husband and wife was "inevitable." For a while, she assumed that once Anthony had made it to the upper echelons of Major League Baseball's elite, there was no way he'd take a simple hometown girl like her with him. Not with the large selection of beauties to which he would be exposed during his extensive travels across the country. But given the history they shared and knowing the parents to which he was born (*both of whom were known for keeping their son grounded*), Doris was not entirely surprised to hear him propose during dinner the night she graduated.

For as long as she had known him, Anthony had been a rather simple, low-maintenance guy, not one to get caught up in all the pomp and circumstance many would assume to be associated with his baseball playing peers. Why he was so focused on the topic of her outward appearance on this particular evening was a total mystery to her.

"Baby, did you forget about A.J.'s school concert tonight?" Anthony asked. "You know he's got his first piano solo."

"Oh my gosh, Anthony," Doris began. "It completely slipped my mind! I've been so caught up dealing with Mama.... Okay, okay, gimme twenty minutes. I'll get it together and we can get outta here."

"Okay," Anthony replied.

"Where is A.J. anyway?" Doris asked. She raced up the stairs to their bedroom while unhooking the banana clip that had been affixed to her head for what seemed like an eternity. As she did so, previously caged clumps that had been confined atop her head began to unfold and cascade down her shoulders and her back with each step she took. Certain pieces continued to fall until they came to rest upon the ground. Maintaining his position at the base of the staircase, Anthony peered down and knelt to retrieve a few of those clumps as moisture began to collect in the corners of his eyes. Then, he answered his wife.

"He left for the concert hall about half an hour ago. He figured that you, I mean we, would need a little more time to get ready, so I sent him on ahead of us with his buddy Timmy Townsend."

"Good!" Doris yelled form the upstairs master bathroom. "This will only take me a few minutes."

"Okay, no worries, babe. We got time," Anthony said. He wiped his eyes, then stared at his wristwatch in a futile attempt to will the second hand to slow down.

Doris gazed into her bathroom mirror, noticing how gaunt her frame had become over the last month. She surveyed the state of her hair with her right hand, liberally distributing full sections of hair so that they covered the bald spots that had begun to reveal themselves.

Less than fifteen minutes later, Doris descended the staircase in full makeup with a grace and elegance that had eluded the creature that bounded up those same stairs a short time earlier. She wore the emerald green off-the-shoulder gown Anthony had given her as a gift on Valentine's Day. Anthony craned his head upward and a smile crept across his face as he beheld the treasure, the gift, God had given him in the form of the brilliant, selfless human being that was his wife.

"I'm glad you wore it down," Anthony said. He gently stroked the outer edges of Doris's hair.

"Gotta take advantage of the opportunity while I can," Doris replied. She smiled and patted Anthony on the cheek. "Let's go see our son."

"After you, Mrs. Tucker," Anthony said. He grabbed his tuxedo jacket, opened the door and placed his hand on the small of Doris's back, while steering her toward the front door. As he did so, the cell phone inside Doris's silver clutch purse began to ring. She removed the phone from her bag, glanced down at the caller ID and swiped her index finger across the lower part of the phone screen to answer it.

"Yes, Delphine?" Doris asked the home health care worker she had hired to provide overnight coverage for Mama a few days prior. While Doris initially felt guilt at the idea of having someone other than herself taking on the responsibility of caring for her ailing mother, with Mama's urging, Doris gave in to the idea of getting external help to provide Doris some well-earned relief in an admittedly stressful situation. Besides, Delphine had come highly recommended and was the epitome of professionalism when it came to taking care of Mama's needs. Delphine also adhered to Mama's admonition that no one outside of the family know about her terminal illness.

Tears began to form in the outer ridges of Doris's eyes as she listened to the words Delphine spoke. Anthony, sensing the news being conveyed could not be good, carefully caressed the back of Doris's head and pulled her close to him. Doris looked up at Anthony, as full-on tears began to stream down her face. She nodded at Anthony in nonverbal communication of the devastating news before she spoke again to Delphine.

"I'll be right there."

"I'm so sorry, babe," Anthony said. He caught the phone that nearly crashed to the ground after Doris's hand slowly descended from her ear.

***

"Her hair looks so good, don't it, girl?" Claudine asked. She glanced down at Mama's impeccably coiffed mane. Claudine also noticed the way the stylishly attired body to which the hair was connected lay stiff in the mahogany casket three feet beneath her as she continued. "Not a strand out of place."

"That's a wig, girl," Sadie whispered to Claudine in reply. "You know they say she had cancer and those chemotherapy treatments and radiation took her hair."

"Aww, poor thing," Claudine said. She elevated her right hand and carefully inserted fingers into the tracks of her weave to scratch the itch that irritated her skull.

"Let's go sit down, girl," Sadie said before Doris began to speak.

***

"As most of you know," Doris began. "Well, many of you may not know because Mama was so notoriously private."

Doris scanned the standing-room-only crowd in search of the strength she would need to make it through Mama's eulogy and found it ten seconds later in the form of Anthony and A.J., who sat in the front row. Doris smiled at them, wiped the tear that had pooled against her right cheek and continued.

"Mama had a form of leukemia which had taken its toll on her in a significant way over the past several months. Many of you wonder why Anthony, A.J., and I have not seen too much of you in these past several months. We hope you will forgive us for being absent from your lives, so we could be that much more present in Mama's. As most of you know, Mama had a way with words. She used to say, 'Doris, no matter what you are going through, never let 'em see you sweat.' She would emphasize the importance of maintaining an outward sense of control in all circumstances. She would say, 'You need to look good no matter what and always, no matter what, keep that hair together.'

And I think one of the main reasons she wanted to keep her illness hidden is that she felt that if people knew she was breaking down physically, this would somehow diminish the image people had of her."

"Well, Mama, I'm here to tell you that all of us in this room know how much beyond the physical you mattered to us. And how strong a woman you were, despite what this illness—an illness I see every day in my work—did to you physically. The illness could not take away or diminish in any way the fact that you pulled yourself together after Daddy died when I was little, moved to this great community and raised me by yourself from the time I was six. That you encouraged the woman speaking these words to believe she could go on to get a degree in nursing despite the financial struggles we faced."

"Or that you imparted in your grandson A.J. an appreciation for music played the right way and taught him the skills you yourself possessed, patiently helping him strike the right piano keys from the time he was four years old. He had his first solo performance the other night, Mama, and he was great. You would have been proud. This is the impact you made. And these are the things that matter—and they have nothing to do with how you looked. Your strength, your wisdom, your courage, lift me up every single day. I take your strength, your wisdom, your courage, and I hope to use all three to help me endure the battle...."

Doris paused before continuing, as she looked over at Anthony and A.J. for comfort.

"To help me endure the battle... that I now face."

At these words, Doris removed her left hand that had been positioned beneath the podium at which she stood and elevated it to reveal the clear plastic bag full of her own hair. Audible gasps filled the sanctuary as she continued.

"In the words of India Arie, 'I am not my hair.' As you can see, some of it rests in this Ziploc bag. I lost these strands over the past couple of weeks and I will lose more as I continue to undergo chemotherapy and radiation. But as it rests in this bag, I stand apart from it right in front of you. Strong and proud. And with the help of family, you all and my doctors, I hope to beat this illness. If not, Mama, I will see you again sooner rather than later," Doris laughed. "If it is in God's will, that would be all right too. But, in the meantime, I'll fight on and try to use this time to make a positive impact in my own way—just as you did."

Doris scanned the crowd until her eyes locked on the tear-soaked ones that gazed back at her from the faces of Claudine and Sadie.

"We are not our hair," she said.

Then, she sat.

FATHERS AND SONS

"Julia, there's a hog in the bed!" Daddy exclaimed.

He lifted the bedspread and looked under it as I lay sandwiched between him and Mama, giggling and gazing up at the extra patch of hair wedged between his ample eyebrows. I was four at the time and my sister Carla, who was six years older, would inform me later that what Daddy sometimes called his face caterpillar in fact was what other grown folks called a unibrow. Whatever it was called, I remember both it and Daddy's comment that night making me laugh so hard that Mama instantly turned toward Daddy, thumped him across the face and shouted.

"Joseph, stop talking crazy and go back to sleep! You know how hard it is to get him to settle down once you get him going." Then, she sank back into her pillow.

She was right. At that age, I was an especially light and restless sleeper, so much so that once I woke up during the night, I rarely could make myself go back to sleep (something I've carried with me into my adult years). There could be no doubt about the accuracy of Mama's statement at that time, but getting back to sleep was the furthest thing from my mind. I was still focused on the statement Daddy had made and the fact that Mama, as usual, managed to suck all the fun out of the room with the flick of her finger and tongue. I leered at Mama who had already fallen asleep again a few seconds earlier. Soon enough, my laughter was replaced by her snoring, which filled the room with the force of a boat engine at full throttle.

Mama always had a way of spoiling my fun with Daddy and, at that age, I saw Daddy's antics as nothing but fun, even though I have distinct recollections of her using the C word to describe Daddy on several other occasions during my childhood. Like the time she walked into the bathroom as Daddy was squeezing Ben Gay on both his toothbrush and mine in preparation for our pre-bedtime ritual ("crazy fool," she'd said), or the time Daddy tried to feed me oatmeal through my ear, telling Mama he could not figure out why I didn't have an appetite ("Man, stop talking crazy," she'd laughed) or the time Mama found Daddy sitting in his rocking chair next to the swimming pool with his fishing pole extended over the water telling me to stop laughing because I might scare away the fish ("Man, you are the craziest person I know!" she'd shouted).

Youth's naivete convinced me that Daddy had designed each of these episodes specifically for my own personal enjoyment, but the reality of Daddy's situation gradually revealed itself as I transitioned into my middle school years. To this day, the events that brought Daddy's "situation" into focus remain emblazoned on my memory.

Everyone, including Daddy, had anticipated my older sister Carla's sweet-sixteen party as though it were the event of the century. Truth be told, there was no way any of us really could avoid feeling that way given the daily reminders Carla slid beneath each of our bedroom doors preceding the big day and the grand proclamation she made to us conveying the importance of the occasion to her. Exactly one month before her sixteenth birthday, the drama began to build in a way that only someone with Carla's sense of style and ingenuity could muster. She made no secret of the expectations she had for that year's party as she scooted her chair from beneath the dining room table that July 30th morning before breakfast, stood, and spoke.

"Today, the countdown to the best day of my life begins. As you all know, exactly fifteen years and eleven months ago, Mama gave birth to the person standing before you. Well, in commemoration of that blessed event, it is my great pleasure to inform each of you—Mama, Daddy, Jeremy—that you all are cordially invited to celebrate with me and sixteen of my closest friends a party like none this town has ever seen!"

Carla always had a way of making every time she opened her mouth seem as though she were addressing a joint session of Congress. I rolled my eyes at the thought of yet another Carla Swanson production. Daddy stared at his daughter curiously like he always did, as though she were an alien from another planet speaking a language no one on Earth could possibly understand without the aid of an interpreter. Mama, on the other hand, beamed with delight. She was so excited that she could not help but interject as Carla spoke.

"Honey, I've already started planning. I called Mrs. Robinson down the street and she has agreed to bake one of her famous four tier masterpieces in honor of the occasion. I've already tabbed several of the hottest catalogs with dresses I think you might like, and I need you to select one as soon as possible so we have enough time to have your measurements taken, place the order and get the dress by the big day. I've already started working on the guest list, I've created a list of party games and...."

At Mama's last statement, Carla raised her hand with her palm facing Mama as if to deflect the words back towards her like a boomerang.

"Mama, I know you mean well," Carla said. "But I want to make my own guest list."

She divided her gaze among Mama, Daddy, and me when she made her next statement.

"Also, I want music only at this party. There will be no party games this year."

These words from Carla appeared to collide head-on with the middle of Daddy's unibrow, which formed a crease and jutted down between his eyes as if to form the letter *V*.

"I completely understand, baby," Mama replied. "I want you to make this birthday whatever you want it to be. You only get one sweet sixteen, after all. And if that means no more pin the tail on the donkey, then so be it."

Daddy, who until that point had remained rooted to his chair picking at his oatmeal, leapt to his feet like a horse breaking from the starting gate.

"No more pin the tail on the donkey!" he exclaimed. "What kind of party is this going to be?"

"Calm down, Joseph," Mama replied. "Your daughter is growing up. She doesn't have to keep playing kids' games if she doesn't want to."

She then turned to Carla.

"When you finish your breakfast, go upstairs and let me know which dresses you like. The catalogs are on my bed."

"Okay, Mama," Carla replied. She turned to exit the dining room.

At the conclusion of their exchange, Daddy sat down and mumbled to himself.

"No more pin the tail on the donkey—we'll just see about that."

"What did you say?" Mama asked.

Daddy did not respond, choosing instead to stare out the window. Mama didn't seem to hear or understand the last statement Daddy made at breakfast that morning, but I did. At that moment, Daddy looked over at me, and when our eyes met, I started to giggle. I could not wait 'til Carla's birthday party.

The days leading up to Carla's birthday party were pretty normal, all things considered. After much deliberation and debate with Mama, Carla finally chose her birthday dress and decided on the party decorations. She completed several run-throughs of the musical selections she had chosen for the party, coordinating the commencement of the first tune with the arrival of the first guest and the conclusion of the last track precisely four hours later. After much discussion with Mama, who previously had limited Carla's birthday gatherings to just three hours with a firm start time and end time, Carla convinced Mama how inherently unfair it was to hold her to such a strict schedule given most people's tendency to arrive at an event "fashionably late," which inevitably minimized the amount of actual party time.

"Why should I be penalized for their rudeness?" Carla had asked. "It would be much more equitable for the clock to begin to run when the first guest arrives."

Under the weight of that statement, Mama relented. Carla even managed to squeeze an extra hour out of Mama utilizing one of her other weapons—her undeniable charm, which she seemed always to reserve for the most special of occasions.

The morning of Carla's sixteenth birthday greeted my ten-year-old body with the faint sounds of plates and glasses clinking together downstairs. I tilted my head in the direction of my Mickey Mouse alarm clock which read 5:45 a.m. and somehow, I just knew the person clamoring downstairs could only be Carla. I tiptoed down the staircase while scooping the remains of sleep from my eyes. My suspicions were confirmed as I glanced around the corner at the edge of the staircase to see Carla's shadow being cast across the kitchen floor.

"What are you doing?" I asked.

"Boy, go back to sleep!" Carla snapped back, as she continued to assemble rows of saucers across the kitchen table.

"I can't," I replied. "You're making too much noise."

"No, I'm not," Carla said. "Don't blame me because you happen to be a life form from another solar system who doesn't know how to sleep through the night."

I responded in a way that only a ten-year-old with an intellect far beyond his years could.

"And don't blame me because you are such a control freak and are so scared things won't work out that you can't relax for one second to allow things to unfold naturally. It's not even six in the morning. What's the matter, Carla? Afraid you'll actually have some *fun* for a change?"

"I hate you!" Carla screamed. She launched a saucer into the air, aiming it directly at my forehead. Luckily for me, my reflexes, like my intellect, had always been quite sharp and I was able to duck instantly so as to avoid what I was convinced at the time would have been certain death.

Mama, on the other hand, was not so lucky. At the precise moment Carla threw the saucer, she rounded the corner and entered the kitchen (no doubt awakened by our shouting) and the saucer made direct contact with her left shoulder, breaking into what seemed like a million pieces. The force of the impact caused Mama to shriek, as she reached for her shoulder with her right hand.

"Jeremy, Carla, get upstairs now!" she exclaimed. "Both of you!"

Carla and I sprinted up the stairs like we were racing for Olympic gold. As Carla closed the door to her bedroom and I entered mine, Daddy stepped into the hallway.

"What happened?" he asked. "Who's screaming?"

"Carla hit Mama with a plate," I said. "I think she's all right, though."

The look of anger that filled Daddy's face is as clear to me today as it was then. Before I could say another word, Daddy shot downstairs like lightning. I have no idea what words were exchanged between him and Mama after that, but the events that followed later that day have stuck with me like a bad, recurring dream that just won't go away no matter how hard I try to make them.

My first thought following the horrible kitchen episode was that Mama (who clearly shared Daddy's anger) immediately would cancel Carla's birthday party as a way to punish her for what happened. I later would learn that Mama had decided not to do so for one reason and one reason alone—some of Mama's relatives from California had flown into town the night before specifically for the party. And how could they not, after Carla—and Mama—had billed the party as the social event of the year. As Mama would say some years later, "I wasn't going to make them waste their money because of that girl's stupidity."

Although the invitations proclaimed a 4:00 p.m. start time, the first guests (who happened to be our out-of-town relatives) arrived at close to 4:30 p.m. Right on cue, Mama started the music as Carla had instructed during their "dress rehearsal" one week earlier. Mama called up the stairs for Carla to confirm there was no last-minute change, but received no answer.

Minutes later, Mr. and Mrs. Stevens from down the street whose daughter Allison was in Carla's geometry class entered the house with gifts in hand. Less than five minutes later, the Foster family from around the corner followed. Little by little, all of Carla's guests trickled in, so that by 6:00 p.m., everyone she had invited had arrived, plus a few who had "gotten the word" from some of those on the "invitation only" list.

"I don't know where that girl is," Mama said in response to Mrs. Foster's query about Carla's whereabouts. Then, she turned to me. "Jeremy, would you please go upstairs to see what's keeping your sister? Tell her that waiting to make a fashionably late entrance is one thing, but being downright rude is quite another thing altogether."

"Okay, Mama," I replied. I paused the race car battle I'd just started with my cousin Justin and bounded up the stairs. Mama's booming voice followed closely behind.

"And tell your Daddy I said to come down here too. I need him to get ready to light the candles."

Just as I landed on the top of the staircase, Daddy exited his and Mama's bedroom. My original plan was to go to Carla's room first, but upon seeing Daddy, I put the question to him instead.

"Daddy, Mama's looking for Carla. Have you seen her?"

Daddy, whose eyes had initially met mine when he left the bedroom, immediately averted his gaze when I asked him the question.

"N-n-no. I don't know where she is," he replied. "Really. I don't know where she is. Sh-she could be anywhere."

"Don't worry, Daddy," I said. "She's probably in her room. I'll just knock on the door. By the way, Mama wants you to come downstairs so you can light the candles."

At those words, Daddy ran downstairs for what I presumed to be the purpose of helping Mama with the party. After ten minutes of intermittent knocking and trying to open a door that was clearly locked, I went back downstairs to inform Mama about my unsuccessful attempt.

"What?!" she exclaimed. "Your sister needs to come down here now! I've had enough of her today!"

She exited the kitchen and began to ascend the stairs.

"Carla!" Mama yelled when she reached Carla's bedroom and began to pound on the door. "Get out here now!"

The deafening silence that greeted Mama caused her to resort to more drastic measures.

"I don't know what's going on with you today, but this is not funny! I'm going to count to five and if you don't come out, you will leave me with no choice."

The absence of sound from the other side of Carla's door continued to thumb its nose at Mama and her counting, as though it had drawn a line in the sand daring her to make the next move. And Mama did.

She went downstairs to the kitchen pantry, removed a hammer from the second shelf and returned, somewhat winded, to the hallway landing just outside of Carla's room. The ease with which Mama dislodged the doorknob to Carla's room with one swing of the hammer would have made any Major League Baseball player proud. Whatever sense of pride that was to be derived from such an impressive display quickly faded when Mama and I caught a glimpse of what awaited us on the other side of Carla's bedroom door.

The image of my sister's limbs pinned firmly against the wall as bloodstained donkey tails dangled from them is as clear today as it was then. The construction paper donkey tail cutouts were firmly fastened against Carla's extremities with nails holding them in place instead of pins. The crimson liquid flowed freely from each nail's point of entry. Carla's head tilted downward and to the right with closed eyes as the partially dislodged piece of duct tape affixed to her mouth moved ever so slightly away from her lips and then back again with each inhalation and exhalation.

"Oh my God!" Mama shrieked. She stared at Carla in shock, not knowing what to do first. She approached Carla's fragile frame. "She's breathing! Jeremy, go call 9-1-1! Use my phone—remember, like we practiced for an emergency!"

The next series of events were quite chaotic and, to this day, remain blurred and jumbled in my mind. I remember running to Mama and Daddy's room, grabbing the phone and dialing 9-1-1 as Mama instructed. I don't remember the amount of time it took for the paramedics to arrive from the time I made the call. I remember the look of horror on one of the paramedic's faces when he entered Carla's bedroom and first eyed her wounds. I remember my aunt from California standing guard at Carla's bedroom to prevent Carla's party guests from coming into Carla's bedroom, then apologizing and instructing them to leave so we could deal with a "family emergency." I remember that it took a few hours to locate Daddy, who I later learned was found holed up inside Mr. and Mrs. Stevens's garden shed sleeping and crouched in the fetal position with a construction paper donkey tail sticking out of his pants pocket.

That was the last day I saw Daddy. That is, until I turned eighteen. For some reason I never understood, the grown-ups wouldn't allow me to see Daddy, no matter how much I consistently begged as I transitioned from childhood to adolescence.

"Daddy's sick" was Mama's reply whenever I asked about Daddy, often followed immediately by an expression of concern that I might "catch" whatever he's got. Every time I pressed the issue concerning the specific nature of Daddy's illness, Mama would just change the subject.

Mama could not shield me from the truth forever, though. Over time, the whispers I initially could not make out as I walked my school hallways grew louder and louder. Suddenly, the C word Mama had so casually sprinkled around the house like the spices she used in her fancy kitchen creations when I was younger became the primary adjective used to describe Daddy by other people in our town. But I refused to believe it. After all, Daddy denied having harmed Carla in any way.

For her part, Carla never spoke about what happened (or, for that matter, pretty much anything else pertaining to Daddy) after her recovery, leaving detectives so utterly perplexed that they were required to draw their own conclusions. For my part, I never told anyone the comment made at the dining room table the month before Carla's birthday party. Nobody ever asked me anything about Daddy at that time anyway. I was always told to leave the room or go outside and play whenever the grown folks had their discussions about "what Daddy did."

I later learned that, when asked why he was sleeping in the Stevens's garden shed, Daddy explained that he got tired while walking down to the pond (which was a block away from the Stevens's home). He said he decided not to attend Carla's party because he believed it was going to be boring since Carla said there would be no party games. Daddy said he had the donkey tail in his pocket in the hopes he would be able to find someone he could play the game with. He then volunteered that he had looked everywhere but could not find the other donkey tails.

Following the days when he had to go to court, Mama sent Daddy to the hospital "so he could rest." She never explained, to my satisfaction anyway, why Daddy could not rest at home.

There was only one place I wanted to be on my eighteenth birthday and I was the first person to arrive when visiting hours at the "adults only" care facility began.

"Daddy, I believe you" were the words that sprang from my lips when I walked into Daddy's bedroom at the place Mama had often described to me as Daddy's second home. I recall being disappointed when Daddy didn't respond to me and instead continued to stare out the window that faced the lake behind the building.

Daddy passed on five years later, but my vivid and fond memories of him have not. They remained strong during those eight years when his physical presence was removed from mine. And they remain just as strong for me this predawn morning as I lay in bed writing these words after my own little boy jostled me awake minutes earlier, while pointing to a round pink object sticking out of my pajama pocket.

"Daddy, there's a hog in the bed!" he exclaimed through giggles.

"I know, son," I replied sleepily, as I removed the plastic little pig Daddy gave me when I was a boy and handed it to him.

"Where'd you get it, Daddy?" he asked.

"My daddy gave it to me a long time ago," I replied.

"Can I have it?"

"Of course, you can, Joey," I said, while rubbing my eyes, knowing I would not be able to get back to sleep.

PURPOSE

WITH GOOD TROUBLE AND JUSTICE FOR ALL

On that Friday afternoon, Phineas Poindexter had wished some wrinkle in the universe would alter past events just enough to spare him the impending physical trauma and humiliation that awaited him. But he knew it was impossible. As much as he wanted to avoid it, he knew it was inevitable that his date with pain would come. Derek Drummond had promised him as much while they stood in the courtyard on the second day of the school year. It was on that second day at precisely 8:47 a.m. that, seemingly out of nowhere, fate had caused the two boys' paths to cross for the first time. Phineas knew he'd been a bit naïve to think his very public stumble across the well-heeled feet of the most popular athlete in school would not set in motion the chain of events that would lead to the jock's promise of violence. He did not know that time, location, and circumstance would also converge to compel the boys to witness an occurrence so profound it would impact them both for life. Phineas recalled the moment of the boys' initial encounter like it was yesterday.

"Dude, I know you did *not* just step on my new kicks!" Drummond yelled.

Laughter sprang from Phineas's lips before he could even register what was happening. When he first perceived Drummond's response to his impromptu appointment with the guy's rubber-soled feet, he was a bit taken aback by the intensity of his reaction. There was no denying that Phineas had unceremoniously smudged Drummond's fresh out of the box, albino white sneakers. But Phineas was somewhat surprised the kid would react so sharply. The year was 2020 and it really was an accident, after all. Phineas had believed maniacal obsessions with basketball shoes for boys of his hue had long faded, like the cheap shoulder tattoo he'd bought a few years prior after finding himself on the losing end of a Boy Scout bet. Phineas vaguely recalled a story his father once told about brawls among boys he grew up with over stolen or damaged pairs of name-brand basketball shoes promoted by some elite NBA players at the time. It was inconceivable to Phineas that any of his contemporaries would engage in such conduct in 2020. Hence, the laughter.

"Nigga, are you laughing?" Drummond asked. "Now I'm gon' have to fuck you up!"

Phineas had moved about ten feet past Drummond by the time he said this, providing just enough space for bodies to wedge themselves between the two boys and interrupting Drummond's effort to make good on his immediate threat.

"Drum, hold up! Hold up!" one of his loyal lieutenants said. "Principal Davis is right over there!"

"Man, you one lucky li'l bitch!" Drummond screamed. "But, come Friday after school, I'm comin' for you! And them's facts!"

Fact. Phineas Poindexter and Derek Drummond were both sixteen years old. Fact. Phineas Poindexter stood five feet six inches tall. He was slight, weighing a whopping one hundred thirty-five pounds while wearing a backpack full of books. The closest he'd ever come to fighting an animate object occurred four years earlier during a disagreement with his family's newly adopted six-month-old German shepherd. They had a difference of opinion over the canine's return trip to her training crate, resulting in a standoff between the two. The German shepherd won. Fact. Derek Drummond stood six feet tall. He was solid and ripped, tipping the scales at close to two hundred pounds in his training sweats. Fights occurred at least four times a month on his watch. He was undefeated. Put simply, he was well-rehearsed.

Phineas's attempts to ready himself in the ensuing days for his near certain demise consisted of prayer and a conversation with his cousin Brent, who'd spent the past two years training in Tae Kwon Do. Phineas's foray into the spiritual realm found him not only with clasped hands and bent knees nightly, but also flipping through passages of the dusty King James Bible he rescued from the depths of a box in the attic. It had been gifted to him by his grandmother when he turned thirteen. He scoured the pages recounting David's improbable triumph over Goliath. When he finished, he closed the book and shook his head. He was convinced Goliath's lack of a reliable weight training facility coupled with the fact that he did not own a sling shot made his odds of victory significantly lower than his biblical counterpart. He found his martial arts conversation with his cousin equally unhelpful.

"Well, as I'm sure you know, cousin, Tae Kwon Do does not depend solely on perfecting sparring, breaking, and other techniques," Brent began. "It is also rooted in the belief that a key path to victory lies in self-defense and self-preservation. You know you're going to face a barrage of incoming, so in anticipation of your foe's attacks, you must always have a counterattack scheme at the ready."

"Counterattack?" Phineas asked.

"Yes, cousin, a counterattack," Brent replied.

"Well, what if his attacks are so vicious that they incapacitate me to the point that I'm unable to mount an effective counterattack?"

"Well, in that case, cousin, you're screwed," Brent replied. "If all else fails, run!"

"Run?" Phineas asked. "You're kidding me, right? The kid runs the anchor leg of our track team's four by one hundred relay. They're the reigning state champions!"

"Okay, then," Brent replied. "Well, in that case, I don't know what to tell you or what advice to give. Other than prayer."

"Well, thank you so much for your sage advice, cousin," Phineas said. "I'll be sure to let you know how it goes. If I happen to live to tell the tale, that is."

"Good luck, cousin," Brent said.

"Yeah, yeah," Phineas replied.

* * *

The day of the big event could not have been more memorable. As the morning bell rang signaling the conclusion of his first period class, Phineas exited his classroom to find two of Drummond's lieutenants standing with their backs against the wall on the opposite side of the corridor. They were waiting for him. They walked five feet behind Phineas as he made his way to his next class.

"Auditioning for the Secret Service, are you?" Phineas asked, loudly enough for the two boys to hear.

Receiving no response to his query, Phineas continued before entering his next class.

"Well, I think you two will make fine candidates. Don't let anybody tell you different."

Phineas punctuated the remaining hours of the school day with similar statements when he changed classes, making every effort to downplay the terror that gripped him from within. The final bell rang precisely at three o'clock, just as Phineas finished emptying his tank of one-liners. By then, he seemed to have slipped away from his escorts. He donned a dark pair of sunglasses and made his way to the outskirts of the courtyard to wait for his school bus. He figured he'd make a run for it as soon as the bus arrived. The sea of humanity that had assembled in the courtyard between him and the parking lot presented a challenge. Just as Phineas began to muster the confidence to make a run for it, he felt a tap on the shoulder.

"You ready?" a lieutenant he thought he'd eluded asked.

Phineas swallowed hard and commenced his stroll to the center of the gladiators' circle. Unlike the day of his first encounter with Drummond, there was no principal in sight to intercede in the event of confrontation. Also, unlike that day, students that had been scattered about the premises quickly encircled him and Drummond en masse, as if they had purchased VIP tickets to the main event at the MGM Grand in Vegas. The only things missing to complete the picture were a cloud of cigarette smoke and cocktails.

Drummond stood a familiar ten feet away from Phineas. He smiled before commencing his approach. As Drummond lifted his right foot to make his advance, a shriek erupted from somewhere in the crowd behind him. In the same instant, a similar howl filled the airspace just a few feet behind Phineas.

Then, another. And another. Waves of students' eyes moved away from the impending fight and toward their smartphones, prompting Drummond and Phineas to grab their devices.

"He's choking the life out of him!" one of Drummond's lieutenants, free from Secret Service duty, exclaimed.

"I can't believe what I'm seeing right now!" the captain of the cheerleading squad yelled. She began to remove tears with her free hand.

"Is this real?" a student asked. "This has to be somebody's idea of a sick joke!"

"It's not a fucking joke!" another student shouted. "This is streaming live! It's happening right now!"

Phineas and Drummond remained in the center of the circle, their feet anchored to the ground. Their mouths fell open as that of the black man on their phone screens shut for the last time. Screams, shouts, and expletives erupted from the bevy of students in reaction to the pleas and protestations that could no longer be heard from the dead man in the video. They continued for what seemed at least an hour until worried parents began to arrive to collect their offspring. A fresh batch of sorrow greeted Phineas when he stepped onto his school bus. Various shades of tear-soaked and angry faces—some black, some white, some brown—kept him company during his forty-five-minute ride home.

* * *

Outstretched maternal arms enveloped and squeezed Phineas when he arrived home. By contrast, his father's remained folded across his chest, as he glared at replayed images of the carnage on the TV screen.

"Thank God, you're home!" Phineas's mother exclaimed. "I've been worried sick. Why didn't you answer your phone when I called?"

Phineas lifted his smartphone and presented its dark screen to his mother.

"Battery's dead," Phineas replied.

"It's not the only thing that's dead," Phineas's father said.

"Mom, Dad," Phineas began, "if it's all right with you, a group of us from the school plan to head downtown later because we feel like we gotta do something to—"

"Absolutely not!" Phineas's mother exclaimed. "You worried me sick all afternoon already! You will *not*—"

"Wait a minute now, babe," Phineas's father interrupted. "Let's hear the boy out, now. Let him talk."

"Well, we just feel like this is not right, Dad," Phineas continued. "And if we don't speak up for him now, who will? It's just not right!"

Phineas removed the charger from his backpack, plugged one end into the wall socket and the other into his phone. His mother shook her head.

"So, who's going down there?" Phineas's father asked.

"Well, right now, it's a lot of us kids from the school. The captain of the cheerleading squad's older sister is organizing it. I think she's connected with that national group that was formed a few years ago after that similar incident in Ferguson, Missouri. They told us we could make signs and bring them if we want, along with bottled water, towels, and other things we might need."

Phineas's father smiled slightly.

"You should know, son, that your mother and I did something similar back during our college days."

"Yes, sir," Phineas replied. "I remember you telling me about the N-word being scratched into the elevator doors of your dorm and the white guys that performed at a talent show in black face."

Phineas's father looked at his mother.

"Your mother and I remember those days like it was yesterday," Phineas's father said. "That was more than twenty years ago. I sure hate you have to go through this and I wish I could say I was surprised it happened at all. But, as I've told you before, this is sometimes the way things go for us. It's definitely not the way it should be, though. And, you're right. Sometimes, it *is* up to us to let folks know it's just not right."

"So, does that mean I can go to the protest?" Phineas asked.

"Yes, you can go," Phineas's father replied. "On one condition."

"What's that, Dad?" Phineas asked.

"That I come with you," Phineas's father replied. "After all, you're my only son, and we just can't risk you being out there by yourself. Well, I know you won't be *by* yourself because your school mates will be there too, but... well, you know what I mean. Your mother would be a wreck."

"Thanks, Dad," Phineas said.

"No problem," Phineas's father replied. "So, what time are we—?"

The ring tone from Phineas's smartphone filled the room before his father could complete his question, prompting Phineas to detach the device from its charger. He glanced at his smartphone's screen, smiled, and steered the phone to his ear.

"So, did you find out what time we're meeting?" Phineas asked.

He paused for five seconds.

"And where?" Phineas asked.

He paused again, dividing his gaze between his father and his mother.

"Got it," Phineas said. "I'll see you there. Later."

"Who was that, son?" Phineas's father asked.

"That was Derek Drummond, captain of the track team and basketball team. We're meeting at six next to Unity Square downtown. So, we probably should leave about thirty minutes before that to make sure we get there on time."

"Okay, sounds good," Phineas's father said. "I'll go change into some more comfortable shoes. Babe, you didn't throw away my old pair of Jordan's did you?"

"No, I didn't," Phineas's mother replied. "They should be under the bed. And while you do that, let me go into the attic. I believe some signs from back in the day might still be hiding behind some old boxes up there. If I blow the dust off them, maybe we can use some of them."

"'*We*'?" Phineas asked.

"Did I stutter?" Phineas's mother replied. "You all are not going down there without me. Now, go ahead and finish charging your phone. Somebody needs to have a way to make a quick call if things get crazy."

"Right," Phineas replied.

He averted his eyes towards his father, who smiled briefly before continuing his walk towards the bedroom to begin searching for his Jordan's.

WONDER WOMEN

To understand how they remained so thin—skeletal really—amidst the seemingly endless array of rice and noodle-laden dishes they effortlessly heaved upon their slender shoulders, whisked from kitchen to dining room and plopped before their often-overweight clientele, Monique knew it would take some ingenuity, skill, and maybe a little luck. Once she had convinced herself that she could, and one day would, know the answer, she slowly began to compose a mental picture of what would be included in what was to become her ultimate investigative masterpiece.

"I knew we could do it," Adrienne said. She gently tapped Sheryl on the elbow with her right hand while pointing to the spot on the ceiling that seemed to capture all of Monique's attention with her left. "Look at her, girl. She's probably already thought of the way to infiltrate their homes with some super-secret spy scope."

"Nice alliteration, Adrienne," Monique said. "You should have been a writer. I think you missed your calling."

As she said this, Monique slowly shifted her focus from the ceiling to both Adrienne and Sheryl, her two sorority sisters who also happened to be her closest friends. Then, the corners of her mouth lifted, revealing a dimpled smile that had been known to stop many a man in his tracks.

"Girl, I think you're right," Sheryl said. "Look at that devilish grin. We've both seen that look before."

"You sure have," Monique replied.

She stood up, gathered her laptop and began to slip on her overcoat.

"I gotta go."

"Where are you going?" Adrienne asked. "We haven't even ordered dessert yet."

Monique continued her preparations to leave, then placed three crisp twenty-dollar bills on the table.

"Dinner's on me," Monique said.

"Adrienne, don't act like you're surprised to see her go," Sheryl said. "You know how she is when she gets in this mode. All I have to say is, look out Christianne Alancour. Somebody's coming for your job. And we only have ourselves to blame."

"Bye, y'all," Monique said. She exited the Korean restaurant she, Adrienne, and Sheryl had frequented at least once a month for the past three years. Inwardly, Monique acknowledged Sheryl was right. For the past six years as she flew from one promotional site to another in furtherance of a high-profile public relations career about which most people her age could only dream, she had no problem admitting to herself (and to those who cared the most about her) that her true passion lay with traditional journalism—investigative journalism to be exact. This was evidenced by the fact that, from time to time, she would funnel fully fact-checked stories she had investigated to the local press (without identifying herself in most instances) only to have them appear on the evening news.

There was also no denying that she harbored a not-so-secret desire to do the type of work that had earned Christianne Alancour of *NCN News* the "chief investigative correspondent" title (Monique was convinced the compelling story Alancour broke about the Abu Ghraib prison scandal—and the images accompanying it—would forever be seared into her memory). But, for now, she would content herself with investigating the "smaller" mysteries that intrigued her, this latest of which had managed to grab her full attention.

Sheryl was also right about another thing. She and Adrienne did have themselves to blame for the question—observation really—that would eventually consume the better part of Monique's fall and winter. As Monique exited the restaurant that crisp fall evening, Sheryl and Adrienne exchanged looks that, without words, communicated the thing they both knew to be true—they would not be seeing their friend very much at all in the coming months. They both knew that once Monique committed herself to a new project, all bets were off.

***

The observation that set the chain of events in motion came from Adrienne while the three were dining at the same Korean restaurant one month earlier.

"Monique, Sheryl. Look around the room at the people in this restaurant," Adrienne said, prompting her friends to lower their forks. They surveyed the people in the dining area. "Most of the folks in here have to be, on average, at least fifteen to twenty pounds overweight."

Sheryl nodded in agreement. Monique gazed down at her own flat midsection, thankful for the high metabolism that accompanied her mid-twenties youth, which kept her in fine form despite the often-unhealthy food selections available to her when she traveled from one city to the next.

"Of course, they're overweight," Sheryl replied. "Look at what they're eating. Most of the meals on the menu are noodle and rice dishes. It's carbohydrate city up in here!"

"Yeah, but now look at the waitresses," Adrienne said. "If these really are traditional Korean dishes, shouldn't the waitresses be eating them? And, if so, how do they stay so thin?"

"That's a good question, girl," Sheryl replied. She shifted her weight and tugged at her sweater hoping to conceal evidence of the additional pounds she had acquired over the past few months. "I wonder how they do it."

"Well, y'all are assuming they actually eat the food they serve here," Monique said. "Maybe that's not a reasonable assumption to make."

"Well, if it's not a reasonable assumption to make, it certainly makes me wonder what they *do* eat when they leave here and go home."

As Adrienne said this, Monique could not help but notice the two Korean waifs (one of whom was their waitress Su-Yin) snickering at each other by the kitchen as they not-so-discretely pointed to an older gentleman who had to be at least five foot nine and two hundred fifty pounds unsuccessfully attempt to shovel mounds of rice between his sauce-stained lips with the assistance of a pair of not-so-cooperative chop sticks. Feeling somewhat sympathetic toward the stranger (as she too was far from skilled at using the tricky eating utensils), Monique immediately knew the observation Adrienne had made in jest would inevitably become her newest project. And she also knew she would not stop until she could rejoin her friends in the future to present them with the answer to Adrienne's question.

* * *

"You don't have to do any heavy lifting with this puppy, that's for sure," Alonzo said. He delicately cradled, then transferred, the tiny gemlike object from the palm of his hand to Monique's. From the start, Monique knew that if she was going to access the home of her newest subject (she had singled out the waitress Su-Yin as her target), she could not do it without some technical know-how and creative skills beyond her own capabilities. And she knew just where to go.

Since the time they were children, Alonzo had always been somewhat of the oddball of his and Monique's friend circle, often choosing to spend hours on end in his make-shift lab (aka his parents' attic) crafting inventions that made him the perennial winner of school science fairs while Monique and the rest of their friends hung out in shopping malls. When Alonzo informed her several years later that he'd landed his dream job doing research and development for IBM, it came as no surprise to her or to any of her friends.

At the moment, she was just thankful she had the good sense to keep the lines of communication with Alonzo open after all these years. She did feel somewhat guilty for exploiting to her advantage the fact that Alonzo had carried a torch for her since they were twelve, but promised herself she would say a few Hail Mary's and donate some time to charity as her own personal penance at some later date. For now, she had work to do. And who better to help in her effort to solve her latest mystery than an old friend? Who needed the internet? She had Alonzo.

"Where'd you get this?" Monique asked. She accepted the device from Alonzo.

"Get?!" Alonzo replied, as if insulted. "I made it. And it is one of my finest creations, if I do say so myself."

"What does it do?" Monique asked. "How does it work?"

"Wait a minute," Alonzo replied. "One question at a time. In response to your first question, I knew that in order for you to make inroads into the inner sanctum of your unsuspecting subject you would have to do so in a stealth-like manner. The only real way to do so would be to devise a scheme whereby you would be able to see what your subject sees and hear what she hears, ideally in real time, without her knowledge."

"I thought what better way to do so than to create an object that would accomplish this goal virtually at your subject's invitation. Now, you tell me, Monique. What young woman struggling to make ends meet serving food every night to sometimes unappreciative customers would turn down an early holiday gift from one of her regular customers—especially a gift that sparkles as brightly as this one will?"

"So, it's a piece of jewelry?" Monique asked.

"Yes, and not just *any* piece of jewelry, my friend—one that shines and changes colors the more one wears it."

"Oh, I see," Monique said. "So, all I need to do is give this 'gift' to Su-Yin and then encourage her to wear it as much as possible—even while at home?"

"You got it," Alonzo replied. "The more she wears it, the more it will shimmer and shine."

"Then, what?" Monique asked.

Alonzo paused for a moment, turned to retrieve from his table a small handheld device that appeared to have a screen of some kind and handed it to Monique.

"That brings me to the answer to your second question," Alonzo said. "When your subject—"

"She has a name, Alonzo," Monique interrupted. "No need to completely objectify the woman. I'm already starting to feel a bit guilty about this as it is."

"Sorry," Alonzo replied. "If you do this right, *Su-Yin* will be so appreciative of the gift and so eager to wear it that she will put it on immediately. To do so, she must snap the clasp on the back. Once the clasp makes contact with the rear of the pendant—and that's what you should call it—the small monitor I'm holding will come to life and will begin to receive from the pendant images of everything Su-Yin sees; assuming, of course, she wears it so that it is fastened to the front of her body. Now, I won't bore you with the technical details of how this happens, but the clasp will initially serve as an activation device, while the camera inside the pendant will be powered remotely by this device I'm holding."

"Understood," Monique replied.

"Now, you'll have to tell her something that will incentivize her to wear the pendant all the time," Alonzo said. "I'll leave that to you. Go ahead, give it a whirl."

As Alonzo completed his statement, Monique adjusted the pendant in her hand so that its rear pointed upwards and its face pointed downward. Then, using her free hand, Monique snapped shut the clasp on the pendant. The moment the clasp clicked shut, the face of the pendant began to glow and Monique felt the beginnings of warmth emanating from the glass. Simultaneously, the monitor Alonzo continued to grasp beeped and immediately sprang to life. Glancing down at the screen of the monitor, Alonzo noticed nothing but darkness. The look of confusion that initially spread across his face changed to comprehension as he realized Monique still had the glass portion of the pendent facing down into her palm.

As he reached into Monique's hand and slowly began to turn the glass portion of the pendent upward revealing vibrant shining colors, images began to appear on the monitor's screen—first, Alonzo's inventor's manual sticking out of the jacket that lay across his chair; next, the *X-Files* poster neatly matted and framed on his wall; and, finally, the stain on his dining room ceiling, which had resulted from his upstairs neighbor's incessant bathroom leaks over the past several months.

"Whoa, that's bright!" Alonzo exclaimed.

"And look at that stain," Monique said as she redirected her focus from the monitor's screen to the ceiling. "I never noticed that before."

"Um, yeah," Alonzo mumbled. "I've got to get that fixed."

"Well, at least we know it works," Monique said.

"Of course, it works," Alonzo replied. "Was there any doubt?"

With that statement, Monique grabbed Alonzo and gave him a peck on the cheek. She stuffed the pendant and monitor inside her purse, gathered her coat and laptop and headed toward the door.

"I can't thank you enough for this!" she exclaimed as she began to exit Alonzo's apartment. "I don't know how I'm ever going to repay you."

"How about dinner some time?" Alonzo asked, as he slowly removed his hand from his still moist cheek, wondering whether she would select a different part of his face next time.

"Uh, I'll get back to you on that," Monique replied, as she headed toward the door.

"Excellent," Alonzo mumbled to himself. He smiled, handed Monique a charger for the monitor, then picked up his TV remote, eager to begin his search for the Discovery channel.

***

The next several weeks proved to be very productive ones for Monique in terms of laying the ground work in anticipation of the day when she would present Su-Yin with her "gift." She ate at the Korean restaurant much more often, each time asking to be seated at one of Su-Yin's tables. More often than not, her requests were granted. Even when they weren't, she made it a point to greet Su-Yin before leaving the restaurant and also did not hesitate to compliment her on her superior service, waiting skills, and even her manner of dress.

Monique also left a sizeable tip before departing the restaurant each time she sat at Su-Yin's tables and, in doing so, began to garner somewhat of a reputation. After a while, Monique didn't even have to request Su-Yin's table. Su-Yin, often over her manager's protests (and once she became familiar with Monique's dining schedule), began to reserve a table in anticipation of Monique's arrivals.

It came as no surprise to the other waitresses or to the restaurant's management when Monique offered Su-Yin what she described as a "small token" of her appreciation for the consistently superior service she received whenever she dined at the restaurant. That did not, however, stop the other waitresses from displaying their obvious jealousy as Su-Yin ripped open the wrapping paper and beamed with delight at the sight of the glass pendent that lay inside the jewelry box.

"Ms. Colton, what is it?" Su-Yin asked. "I've never seen anything like it before."

"First, how many times do I have to tell you Su-Yin?" Monique asked, smiling. "My name is Monique. My mother is Ms. Colton."

"Oh, sorry," Su-Yin replied. "I always forget. Please tell me what it is."

"It's a pendant, Su-Yin," Monique replied. "It's transparent and clear now, but just wait until it starts to glow when you try it on. Why don't you put it on now?"

Su-Yin happily obliged. The clumsy manner with which she extracted the object from the box quickly turned to grace as she gingerly elevated the object to the front of her blouse. With one swift motion, Su-Yin affixed the glass front of the pendant to her shirt with one hand and with the flick of the thumb from her other hand snapped the clasp shut. Su-Yin flinched briefly when the rear of the clasp made contact with her chest after she removed her thumb.

"Oh, that's cold," she said.

As it did many weeks before in Alonzo's apartment, the face of the pendant began to glow, first appearing to be a bright yellow, then a shimmering green and it continued to change colors at random. Monique cleared her throat to conceal the faint beeping sound from the monitor inside her purse.

"Are you okay?" Su-Yin asked.

"Yes, I'm fine," Monique replied.

"Ooh, I've never seen anything quite like this!" Su-Yin exclaimed. "It's so beautiful. Where did you get it?"

The other waitresses—unable to contain their curiosity—gathered around and gazed at the pendant in amazement.

"Well, you remember when I told you about the photo shoot I had to attend for my company in Miami?"

"Yes," Si-Yin replied.

"Have you ever been there?" Monique asked.

"No," Su-Yin replied.

"Good, I mean, well I picked it up at a little shop in an area of the city called Coconut Grove," Monique said. "They have some of the most unique pieces of jewelry I have ever seen. I saw this and immediately thought of you."

"Wow!" Su-Yin replied. "This is so special. Thank you so much for this."

At that moment, a tear began to well in Su-Yin's eyes and it took all the strength within Monique to shield herself from the avalanche of guilt that threatened to descend upon her at the thought of her deception. Monique quickly realized that, guilt or not, she had come too far to turn back. Besides, the pangs of guilt she felt at that moment paled in comparison to the overwhelming sense of curiosity that grew within her from the day Adrienne asked the question. Monique knew she would soon have her answer.

"Does it operate on batteries or anything?" Su-Yin asked.

"No. It is heat sensitive," Monique replied. "The closer you have it to your body, the brighter it will glow. I was told that each time you secure the clasp, the pendant will start to glow, but to maintain the glow, keep it close to your body—for example, against your chest like you have it now—because the heat from your body will cause it to maintain its shimmer and shine."

"I understand," Su-Yin said. "I don't think I will ever take it off then."

Monique smiled.

* * *

Several months and therapy sessions later, Monique slowly began to dig herself out of the grave of guilt that had buried her. With each image she saw of the desperate Korean refugees to whom Su-Yin and the other waitresses dutifully transported leftovers from the restaurant, Monique became more and more depressed. Every night after the restaurant closed, Su-Yin and the other waitresses traveled to the outskirts of town to deliver food. Monique cringed—and, in some instances, wept—with each image she observed. Although she could not understand the language to know the specific circumstances that led the refugees to their wretched state of existence, Monique gleaned enough information from the visual footage to know that, whatever the circumstances, they were far from good.

As horrible as the refugees' plight appeared to be, Monique could not help but be amazed by the compassion and commitment exhibited by Su-Yin and her fellow waitresses as they ended their shifts at 11:30 p.m. and then, after their restaurant cleaning rituals, drove sometimes an hour and a half to the various locations where the refugees were housed, many of which appeared to be abandoned underground bunkers or bomb shelters that had been converted to makeshift living quarters.

What appeared to be spaces of no more than one thousand square feet sometimes housed as many as fifty people at a time with varying levels of personal hygiene. Monique recalled becoming physically ill at the sight of a dust laden toddler unintentionally crushing the outstretched arm of what appeared to be his sleeping sibling as he hurried toward Su-Yin when she approached with a tray of rice and vegetables. Monique wondered how long it had been since the child had eaten as he—and the other occupants of that particular shelter—devoured the contents of Su-Yin's tray within ten minutes.

Monique shook her head in disgust as she watched the picture on the monitor fade to black each night when Su-Yin collapsed at the table of food she had prepared for herself—sometimes after 3:00 a.m.—after having worked at the restaurant and then delivering food to the refugees only to wake the next morning to repeat the cycle.

* * *

"Hey, girl," Adrienne said.

She gave Monique a peck on the cheek while sitting at Su-Yin's table at the Korean restaurant during the lunch rush. "Have you been working out? You look like you have lost some weight."

"No," Monique replied. "I guess I just haven't been eating well lately."

"Why not?" Adrienne asked. "What's wrong?"

"Nothing's wrong with *me*," Monique replied, as an extra layer of moisture gathered in her eyes while she stared at Su-Yin. "Nothing at all."

"You remember when we were last here together—you, Sheryl, and me?" Monique asked.

"It's been several months, but yes, of course I do," Adrienne replied. "And I'm sure something we discussed on that day is probably the reason I haven't heard from you in so long."

"Well, you're right. Either you or Sheryl wondered what the waitresses here eat to stay so thin."

"That was me," Adrienne replied. "And, now that I think on it a bit more, that was almost eleven months ago. The last time the three of us were here together, you seemed to be daydreaming during most of the meal and then you left early."

"Here," Monique said.

She shoved a miniature thumb drive into her friend's hands.

"You can't tell anybody about this, Adrienne. Not until I figure out what to do."

"Tell anybody about what?" Adrienne asked.

She gazed down at the USB.

"Just promise me, Adrienne," Monique said.

She stood up and began to exit the restaurant while placing two twenty-dollar bills on the table.

"Okay, I promise," Adrienne said. "Where are you going?"

***

Monique was reminded what day it was when she pressed the Play button on her answering machine. On the day she returned from her week-long California promotional tour, Su-Yin's plight and that of the people she served continued to preoccupy her to the point where she simply had forgotten. It was August 7th—her birthday. The first message was from Adrienne and it was left on the machine three days earlier.

I know you're out of town. I also know your birthday's coming in a few days, girl, so happy almost birthday. I've done something and I sure hope you don't get mad at me. Just be sure to watch the NCN news on August 7 at 6:30 p.m. But, if you're not home by then, don't worry because I'm recording it.

As Monique listened to the machine, she glanced down at the clock on her cable box, which read 6:29. She pressed the Pause button on her answering machine and then pressed the Power button on her TV remote. As she entered the numbers for NCN, Monique heard the familiar musical introduction to the news program and viewed the headlines on the TV screen. The first two headlines focused on familiar topics—the war in Iraq and the President's illegal telephone eavesdropping policy. The third topic intrigued her and spotlighted a subject with which she had become intimately familiar. The headline read "Wonder Women." The news anchors commentary followed:

Korean refugees in our midst and the women who care for them—how did they get here and, now that they are, what happens next?

Monique patiently waited through the first stories and then stared at the TV with her mouth agape, mesmerized as Christianne Alancour reported on the deplorable conditions in which the familiar faces she had observed over the past several months found themselves. Alancour used footage Monique had given to Adrienne to give light and life to her story, she featured an interview with Su-Yin and some of the other waitresses from the restaurant, who talked about how they single-handedly kept the refugees alive through their efforts. Alancour ended the piece with commentary about how the individuals appeared to have fled North Korea with the aid of a network of underground contacts in fear of political persecution for speaking out against the country's leader and, as such, likely would be permitted to remain in the United States after being processed through the Immigration and Naturalization Service.

As the piece ended, Monique wiped tears that had gathered in her left eye and then pressed the Off button on her TV remote. As she did so, the phone rang.

"Hello," Monique said. She adjusted the receiver to her ear.

"Ms. Colton, this is Christianne Alancour with *NCN News*. I've been trying to reach you for several days now. I hope you received my messages. I'd like to talk to you about your Korean refugee footage and, if you don't mind, also about your career."

Monique continued to hold the phone receiver to her ear and she glanced over at the answering machine. As the Pause button continued to flash, the corners of her mouth curled upward as a familiar dimpled smile slowly crept across her face.

WHO YOU KNOW

Road weary and hung over, the self-proclaimed "best rapper alive" slumps over the penultimate row of the decidedly less-than-swank vehicle his manager reserved for him three days prior. The rental car companies fronting the regional airport at which the rapper's private jet landed lacked the high-end road transportation options to which the rapper had become accustomed. In lieu of luxury limousine accommodations, on this particular night, a lesser quality minivan would have to shepherd him from aircraft to hotel.

"What is this?" the rapper asked. "The soccer mom deluxe?"

The rapper is far from enthusiastic about making the charity appearance orchestrated by the man whose loins created him. He has no real relationship with the man. His antipathy towards the man is understandable. His father's conspicuous absence from his life and that of his white Jewish mother for the better part of the rapper's existence has made an indelible imprint upon him. Knowing he is but one of many children the man sired with various women both before and after his birth fuels his dislike, not to mention his art. Much like the circumstances the rapper suspects were the inspiration for the catchy and much-praised Temptations song that preceded him by decades (the metaphorically brilliant one about "papas" and "rolling stones"), more than a few of the rapper's hits feature lyrics fiercely lamenting the challenges he, like many of his fans, faced in the absence of a father during his formative years.

While some would think the circumstances providing fodder to help him amass millions might make the rapper re-think his feelings towards the man or perhaps at the very least give him reason to be okay about doing this one thing in return, they do not. It was his mother's protestations to do the charity event in the still-struggling home city of his father and the rapper's "other extended family" (with whom he has no real connection) that swayed him. She reminded him of his humble beginnings and focused him on the bigger picture. She convinced him that doing the charity event would not only benefit the community, but also positively impact his bad-boy image.

"Don't get so caught up in the glitz and glamour to the point where you can't remember the days we'd sell my homemade jewelry on the weekends to get the extra cash to buy bus fare so you could go to your auditions and music competitions," she'd said. "And, as for your father, though I wish things had been different, I could never hate the man. After all, he gave me you."

"Okay, okay, Mom," the rapper had replied. "I'll do the show!"

Five years and two hundred million dollars since being crowned the winner of the most popular reality show competition in the country, the rapper can afford a fleet of buses to transport hundreds of struggling artists towards their dreams. In his case, he knows how blessed he is to have a mother who sacrificed to provide opportunities for him to soar. And, if she could forgive the man who, quite literally, helped create him, he wonders why he cannot find it within himself to do so. As he continues to ponder this in his still-inebriated state, he takes solace in knowing that, at a minimum, he has risen above his complicated feelings about the man and agreed to the charity gig.

"Where in the *fuck* are we?" the rapper's driver asks. He steers the minivan swiftly around the boulder-sized road kill adorning the dirt road. The rapper's six-foot two-inch frame meets the right interior side panel as the vehicle swerves left, jolting him from semi-conscious to fully awake.

"What happened?" the rapper asks.

"We almost crashed into a, uh, uh, I don't know what the fuck that was, bruh!" the driver exclaims.

The rapper quickly turns, facing the rear of the vehicle. He looks out the back window.

"Holy shit!" the rapper exclaims. "That thing was huge!"

"I told you," the driver replies. "And I almost hit it. Thank God for headlights. I ain't seen a street light since we left the airport. It's pitch black out here!"

"I know, man," the rapper says. "Just take it slow. Especially in this piece of shit car. What are we riding in anyway?"

"Man, I don't know what the hell this is," the driver laughs. "I just hope we make it to the hotel in one piece."

The rapper's head is a fraction of an inch from the backside of the driver's headrest. He lowers it. He unfolds the bend in his legs, allowing them to extend across the length of the back seat. He closes his eyes in search of a few more minutes of shut-eye. He hears the sirens.

"What now, bruh!?" the driver exclaims. He sees the flashing red and blue lights in the rearview mirror. "It's five-O!"

"What!?" the rapper asks. He rises in an instant, placing both his feet against the floorboard and his back against the seat. Even though he's not driving, instinct compels him to sink his right hand into his pocket and extract the mints he swiped from the jet before deplaning. He pops them into his mouth.

"It's the police, man," the driver replies.

"The police! Why?" the rapper asks.

"Bruh, I don't know," the driver says.

"A'ight, a'ight," the rapper says. "It's cool. It's cool. We ain't done shit, so it's all good. You didn't have nothin' to drink on the plane, did you?"

"Nah, man," the driver says. "You know we talked about that. Not when I know I'm gonna drive."

"A'ight, cool," the rapper says. "Then, just pull over. It'll be cool."

The minivan slows to a crawl. It stops between two large pines that line the dirt road. The rapper looks over his left shoulder, then through the headlight-illuminated dusty haze to see the police car. The officer opens his car door. He exits the vehicle. He caresses his revolver. He moves slowly towards the passenger side of the minivan.

"Keep your hands on the steering wheel and *do not* move them," the rapper whispers to the driver. The rapper slowly raises his own hands, placing one on either side of the back of the driver's side head rest.

The officer taps the driver's side window, startling the driver.

"What do I do?" the driver asks. Sweat beads form at his temples, then travel down his cheekbones to his chin. He fights the urge to wipe them off.

"Open the window!" the rapper exclaims.

"But I thought you said not to move my—"

"Bruh, just open the damn window! Then, put your hand back on the wheel!" the rapper exclaims.

"Oh, okay," the driver replies.

The window glass lowers, as does the temperature of the minivan's interior when crisp fall air wafts inside.

"License and registration, please," the baritone-voiced officer growls, his thick Southern drawl on full display.

The driver freezes, momentarily. Nerves journey from his inner regions to his hands and make them tremble against the steering wheel.

"Uh, I have my license, but, uh, this a rental car, so I don't know where the registration …."

"Inside the glove box!" the rapper exclaims.

"Go ahead," the officer says.

The driver removes his right hand from the steering wheel, leaving a film of perspiration behind. He reaches for the glove box. He unhooks its latch. He removes the registration and hands it to the officer.

"And your license?" the officer says.

"Uh, oh yeah," the driver replies. His left hand continues to clasp the steering wheel, while he guides his right hand towards his back pocket, lifts his wallet and flips it open. He pushes his license outside the window. The officer aims his flashlight toward the license.

"Casper Wilson from New York City," the officer says. "We don't get many of your kind in these parts. What brings you to town?"

"Um, we're here for a concert, sir," the driver replies.

"A concert, huh?" the officer asks. "Whose concert? I ain't heard nothin' 'bout no concert comin' up."

"Uh, Dragon Dre'," the driver replies.

"Dragon, Dre'," the officer says. "I ain't never heard of no Dragon Dre'. What kind of music they play?"

"Uh, hip hop," the driver replies. "He a rapper."

The driver rotates his head. He faces the rapper who remains still and quiet in the back seat.

"Wait a minute," the officer says. He aims his flashlight towards the back seat. "He talkin' 'bout you?"

White light floods the rapper's pupils. He squints and raises his right hand to shield himself from the onslaught.

"Yes, sir," the rapper replies.

"Let me see your license," the officer says.

"My license?" the rapper asks.

"Did I stutter?" the officer replies. "Yes, your license."

"What did *I* do?" the rapper asks.

"Get out the car!" the officer exclaims.

"What?!" the rapper replies. The driver lowers his head until it hovers just above the steering wheel. He shakes it from side to side.

The officer caresses the butt of the revolver that protrudes from the holster strapped at his right hip. He unclasps the holster.

"I said get out of the car!" the officer exclaims. "Both of you!"

The rapper removes his hands from the driver's headrest, opens the minivan's back door and swings his legs to the left so that they, together with his feet, dangle outside. He stands up just outside the door. He turns to his right. He looks inside the vehicle and makes eye contact with the driver. He nods his head in an effort to coax the driver to join him outside. The driver looks at the red-faced officer, noticing the name on his badge—"*Thibedeau.*" He also notices the officer's hand remains affixed to his weapon. He exits the vehicle.

"You both are under arrest."

"Arrest?" the rapper asks.

Sweat drips freely from the driver's forehead.

"You heard what I said," the officer replies. "You are under arrest."

"Arrest for what?" the rapper asks.

"You're under arrest for hitting one of our most endangered species and leaving the scene of the crime."

"What?!" the rapper exclaims. "C'mon, man. We didn't hit nothin'. That thing was already dead. We just missed it when we was driving down the—"

"Turn around!" the officer exclaims. "Both of you. And put your hands on the vehicle!"

The officer guides his left hand towards his waist, lifts two pairs of handcuffs and proceeds to use them. He escorts both men to his cruiser.

"Now, get in the car!"

The rapper and driver comply. The officer turns his car around, then glides around and past the carnage in the road en route to police headquarters. The two men's heads swivel, then look through the back window as they pass the bloody, mangled mess in the road. They face each other and wonder what's next.

***

"You look familiar," the heavy set, caramel-hued female intake officer at headquarters says. "Face front."

The rapper faces the camera. A click. A flash. The rapper blinks.

"Turn left," the intake officer says.

The rapper faces left. A click. A flash. The rapper blinks.

"Turn right," the intake officer says.

The rapper faces right. A click. A flash. The rapper blinks.

The intake officer repeats the process with the driver. She then proceeds to fingerprint both men. She begins to escort them to a jail cell. The rapper speaks.

"What about a phone call?" he asks. "Don't I get a phone call or something?"

"Oh, yeah," the intake officer replies. "Over here."

She guides the rapper to her desk. She extends her hand toward the old school phone anchored to her desk. The rapper takes a deep breath and slowly exhales. He loathes the thought of having to call. He pauses again before lifting the phone's receiver and dials. The chord connecting the receiver to the phone's base unravels and extends as the rapper presses the receiver against his ear. Disappointed by the absence of a live voice on the other end of the receiver, at the sound of the high-pitched beep the rapper leaves a long-winded voicemail message in response to the pre-recorded voice on the other end.

***

It is 1:30 a.m. The seasoned criminal defense lawyer's smartphone rings silently, vibrates and buzzes. With each vibration, the phone travels ever-so-slightly across the edge of his nightstand. On the third vibration, it reaches the edge of the nightstand. On the fourth, it tips over the nightstand's edge and journeys downward. It meets the hardwood floor with a loud thud. The lawyer's eyes pop open. He extends his hand from beneath the down comforter. He reaches down to scoop up the phone. He taps the phone's screen and presses the device to his right ear.

"Hello," he says. He pauses.

"Yes, I'm awake," he continues. He pauses.
"Uh-huh, uh-huh," he says.
He swings his legs over the side of his bed and stands.
"Who's been arrested? Can you repeat the name?"
The lawyer's eyes open fully. The volume of his voice rises.
"And what was the charge?"
The lawyer smirks. He shakes his head.
"And what are the grounds?"
He pauses.
"I'll be right there," the lawyer says. "Give me a couple of hours, though. I need to make a call and a quick stop before I head over there."
"Who was that, babe?" the lawyer's wife asks. She twists her frame and positions her head on the large goose down pillow upon which it rests to face him.
"Someone I haven't heard from in years," the lawyer replies. "There's been an arrest. Two bruthas accused of doing wrong. So, I need to head out."
"Now?" the wife asks. "It's the middle of the night."
"I know," the lawyer replies. "Timing's bad. But, the arraignment's first thing in the morning, so I need to go. Probably not a big deal, but I do need to head out. Hopefully, I'll be back soon. Kiss the girls for me before they head to school if I'm not back by morning."
"Be careful," the wife replies.
"I will," the lawyer says.

* * *

"All rise!" the bailiff bellows "Oye, oye, oye! All those having business before the Court of the sixth district in the fourteenth judicial circuit in and for Oopsaloosa County, Alabama, please draw nigh. The Honorable Allison Shenshaw presiding."
The door behind the bench separates from its latch. Judge Shenshaw breezes through the threshold and steps up to the bench. She folds herself into her high-backed leather chair, tucks the wayward wisps of blonde locks behind her left ear and speaks.
"Please be seated."
The rapper and the driver sit stock still in two of the three chairs positioned behind defense counsel's table. The third seat remains empty.
"We are here on the matter of the State of Alabama versus Andrew Grantham and Casper Wilson. Will counsel announce their appearances, please?"
"Tracy Heather Benson for the State, Your Honor," the lawyer at the prosecutor's counsel's table says.

Officer Thibedeau stands by her side. He smiles.

Moments after Benson concludes her statement, double doors at the rear of the courtroom fly open. An impeccably attired Deandre Payne steps into the high-ceilinged tribunal and makes his way to the empty seat behind defense counsel's table.

"Nice to see you could join us, counsel," Judge Shenshaw says. "Still cutting it close, I see. I guess some things never change."

She smiles.

"My apologies, Your Honor," Payne replies. "I had to make an important stop before my arrival. I was just retained to handle this matter last night. I appreciate Your Honor's patience."

"No need to apologize, counsel," Judge Shenshaw says. "I said you were cutting it close. You're not late. We're just getting started with appearances. Ms. Benson just announced her appearance for the State, so...."

"Of course, Judge," Payne replies. Standing behind defense counsel's table, he clears his throat.

"Deandre Payne for defendants Grantham and Wilson, Your Honor."

"We are here today for the arraignment of Defendants Andrew Grantham and Casper Wilson," Judge Shenshaw says.

Payne urges his clients to stand. They oblige.

"Mr. Grantham, Mr. Wilson you have been charged with the unlawful killing of an endangered species and leaving the scene of the crime. How do you plead?"

Payne leans over and whispers to his new clients.

"Not guilty, Your Honor," Grantham says.

"Not guilty, Your Honor," Wilson says.

"All right, then," Judge Shenshaw replies. She turns to her right and begins to tap a few keystrokes on her laptop. She stares at her monitor. "Well, I'm looking at my calendar and it appears the next available slot of four days is nine months from now. I believe that should be enough for you all to complete discovery and four days should be more than enough time to try this case, shouldn't it?"

"It should," Benson replies.

"Your Honor?" Payne says.

"Yes, counsel," Judge Shenshaw replies.

"May I approach?"

"Of course," Judge Shenshaw replies. Payne strolls into the well of the courtroom and approaches the bench with a manila folder tucked beneath his arm. He is followed closely by Benson.

The rapper and the driver sit quietly behind defense counsel's table, while Office Thibedeau does the same at prosecutor's table. Ten minutes elapse.

Payne opens the manila folder, extracts items from it and whispers to the judge with intermittent objections by Benson. Benson spins angrily in her three-inch heels and stomps back to the prosecutor's table. Payne walks calmly towards defense counsel's table with the beginning of a smile on his face.

"Will the defendants rise, please?" Judge Shenshaw asks. She stares angrily at Officer Thibedeau.

Grantham and Wilson stand alongside Payne.

"Upon taking judicial notice of additional information that just came to my attention in this matter, I hereby dismiss all charges against defendants Grantham and Wilson."

She looks directly at Grantham and Wilson.

"You are free to go."

"Yes!" Grantham exclaims.

"Officer Thibedeau," Judge Shenshaw says. "I need to see you in my chambers right now, sir."

Officer Thibedeau walks reluctantly into the well of the courtroom towards the bailiff where he waits to be escorted into the judge's chambers.

"We are adjourned," Judge Shenshaw says.

The rapper then turns to Payne.

"My man," he says. "Whatever you said to her, man. I can't thank you enough for coming to my rescue."

He turns to the driver.

"I mean, to *our* rescue. And on such short notice too, man. How did you—"

"Your dad called me last night and hired me," Payne replies. "It's all good. I'm just glad it worked out for you guys."

"But, how did you do it?" Grantham asks.

"Well, Alabama's got a lot of out-of-date laws on the books, but, for the life of me, I could not find one that makes it a crime to run into an opossum."

"Wait a minute, that officer told us we hit some endangered species or something," Grantham says.

"Well, that was a lie," Payne replies. "Unfortunately, there's nothing 'endangered' about our opossum population."

"But that thing we almost hit was huge," Wilson says. "That was an opossum?"

"Yep, it was. Here's the picture to prove it. Apparently, our opossums have appetites about as big as the rats in New York City."

"I see," Grantham replies. "And we didn't hit that thing, anyway...."

"No, you didn't," Payne says. "And that was the other key to our success today."

He removes from his recently accessed manila folder a set of photos and places them in front of Grantham and Wilson.

"As you can see, there were no dents or marks or traces of blood of any kind on your vehicle. If you'd hit that thing, that mangled mess of an animal surely would have left something behind as far as I'm concerned."

"Man, you had a busy night," the rapper says. "How can I repay you, man?"

"Don't worry about that," Payne says. "Your dad's got me covered. He's got my hourly rate. It's all good."

"But, man, c'mon—" the rapper replies.

"No, really," Payne says. "I'm good. I just hope you don't let this experience color your overall impression of us here in Oopsaloosa County. While it's true we've got some bad apples that are trying to drag us back in time like good old Officer Thibedeau did, there are many more of us in this town who are trying to do the right thing and move us forward."

"True, 'dat," Grantham replies. "Well, thanks again, man."

"My pleasure," Payne says. "Now, you fellas hold tight here. When the bailiff comes back, he'll take you to get your phones, wallets, and the rest of your stuff."

Payne shakes Wilson's hand and then Grantham's. He approaches the double doors at the rear of the courtroom, turns towards Grantham and speaks.

"It was good to see you again, man."

Payne notices Grantham already high-fiving Wilson in relief from having just dodged a bullet. He smiles and exits.

* * *

Less than a minute after retrieving his smartphone, Grantham speed dials the person he last called before it was taken from him. This time a live voice meets his.

"Hello?"

"Man, whoever put you in touch with that lawyer deserves a medal," Grantham begins.

His father smiles.

"And do you know he didn't want anything from me even when I offered?"

"Well, he's doing all right for himself," Grantham's father says. "He's well-respected around here and he's built a nice practice for himself."

"But I'm still trying to figure out why he would do something like this for someone he doesn't even know. I mean, he stepped up like that in less than twenty-four hours! You must have told him who I was, right? But then again, he didn't want my autograph or a pic or anything, so maybe you didn't tell him and he doesn't know?"

A long pause. Grantham continued.

"But why would someone do what he did—get up out of his bed in the middle of the night—to help someone he doesn't even know?"

"Well, number one, that's how folks—*our* folks—are around here. I know you don't remember that because you haven't been back in this town since your mom let me bring you down here when you were a little boy," Grantham's father says. "And number two, this guy has a reputation for going to the mat for his clients and I'm pretty sure it's even more so when it comes to family, even distant family."

"Family?" Grantham asks. "What do you mean, *family?*"

***

Deandre Payne crosses the threshold of his home and is immediately greeted by his wife.

"How did it go today?" she asks.

"It went well, babe," Payne replies. "We won!"

"Congrats, babe," Payne's wife says.

"Thanks."

"You must be exhausted," Payne's wife says. "After all, you barely got a few hours' sleep last night."

"By the way," Payne's wife continues. "Your daughters came to me earlier today and you know what they asked me about? I'll give you one guess."

"I don't have to guess, I know," Payne replies. "The Dragon Dre' concert."

"Babe, you've kept this secret from them for long enough, don't you think? They're teenagers now. And he's in town for a special charity concert event that's already sold out, of course. He *never* comes here, even though he has family ties."

She continues.

"Now, I understand why you haven't told them your cousin's half brother is one of the biggest rap stars on the planet—you don't want people to befriend them just because of who they know, and—"

"Fine," Payne replies.

His wife continues.

"And I know that even though you have this distant connection, you don't really *know* him...."

She pauses.

"Wait a minute," she says. "Did you just say 'fine'?"

"I did," Payne replies. He smiles.

"What does *'fine'* mean?" she asks.

"It means I'll make a couple of calls and see what I can do."

"Babe, I know it's probably a long shot," his wife says. "But if you can make this happen, your daughters will be so excited!"

She wraps her hands around Payne's waist and squeezes. Payne glances over his wife's right shoulder. His eyes rest upon the small black and white framed photo positioned atop the fireplace mantel. Though somewhat faded, he can still make out the faces of the two boys who accompanied him on the fishing trip all those years ago—his cousin's with a smile as bright as the sun and that of his cousin's scrawny Yarmulke capped half brother from up north, with something less than a smile on his.

THE FORK

Muted and muffled. Eyes down. Boy adjusts backpack and begins his brisk one-and-a-half-mile trek from home to middle school. Bare toes extend and expose themselves to elements like tortoise exiting hard shell shelter at daybreak. Foot digits dangle slightly over lips of rubber-soled Converse. A bead of moisture rounds, drops, meets pinky toe.
Did that come from me? Teddy thinks. *Or was it a drop of rain?*
He recalls how overcast it was when he first peeked outside his bedroom window to perceive sky. His focus shifts swiftly from pavement cracks to creamsicle-colored rays that spill beyond clouds.
Nope. No rain yet, Teddy thinks. *But it's only a matter of time.*
It is springtime in South Florida.
Eyes move back down again. A second droplet connects with big toe, then a third, transforming suspicion to confirmation.
Yep. It's me, Teddy thinks. Brow perspiration. Nerves.
"Pull yourself together!" Teddy mouths to himself. He quickly steps toward school's main doors. "Only a few feet more."
"A few feet!" the voice exclaims, index finger pointing to Teddy's recently altered footwear. "A few toes is more like it!"
"Dammit!" Teddy exclaims. A chorus of laughter rains down much harder than the storm he managed to escape ever could. "I was so close."
But close to what? Teddy thinks to himself.
Only a matter of time for the world eventually to witness this latest example of his low-income status. Better to remove the bandage slowly or to rip it off with one painful, but swift, motion? Why avoid the inevitable? In the end, isn't this the better result?
The end? Teddy thinks. *Or is it only just the beginning?*
"Love the new look, loser," Tommy Hicks says. "But where's the heel? When my mom's toes are showing in the front, there's usually a high heel in the back!"
Guffaws abound.
"Yeah, yeah, Hicks," Teddy retorts. "Your mom told me to stop by later so she can finish the job she started last night. I guess I'll let her."
A brief moment of silence. Surprise? Teddy surveys the crowd, smirks, briefly takes offense.
C'mon guys, Teddy thinks. *That was a good one!*
Another pause precedes hyena howls and bodies bent at the waist, doubled over. Fingers point to baby faced, beet-red Tommy Hicks. Teddy smiles.
A punch. Pain. Darkness.

Pungent odor. Bitter taste in mouth. Mumbling voices. Cold towel to forehead. Then, light.

"Good," Nurse Campbell coos, inspects Teddy's eyes and forehead. She places smelling salts on desk. "He's opened his eyes—finally. And there's not much bruising. Thank God!"

"Theodore Willis," Principal Sims says. "I am so glad you could awake from your slumber to join the land of the living again."

"Anything for you, sir," Teddy whispers. Sarcasm.

"Sense of humor's intact, I see," Principal Sims retorts. "Thank you kindly, Nurse Campbell. We should be okay now."

She exits office.

"Did someone carry me here?" Teddy asks, mystified by events causing his body to move from one location to the next. He discounts teleportation as a realistic possibility.

"I did," Principal Sims replies.

"Um, thanks?" His voice elevates, resets to normal.

"Ah, it was nothing," Principal Sims says. "Anything for you, sport."

Principal Sims closes his eyes briefly, mentally dispenses self-congratulatory pat on the back for effectively employing technique encouraged by recently read *Bridge Building Bible for Education Professionals.*

CHAPTER 1—BECOME THE STUDENT'S FRIEND; IT IS THE TRUE PATH TO BUILDING TRUST EN ROUTE TO ACADEMIC EXCELLENCE.

"Now, about those shoes," Principal Sims continues.

"If it's all the same to you, sir, I don't want to talk about it."

"Did anyone in this room ask Teddy Willis to talk about anything?" Principal Sims asks, scans the room, hands elevated.

"Sir, we're the only two people in the room," Teddy replies.

"I guess that means the answer's no, then," Principal Sims replies. "Because I sure didn't ask Teddy Willis to says anything, and I'm sure you didn't ask Teddy Willis to—"

"Okay, sir, okay," Teddy says.

"So, as I was saying, about those shoes," Principal Sims continues. "Let me see. Where did I put that thing?"

Principal Sims rises slowly, removing himself from chair behind his desk. He approaches the bookshelf, extracts slender, leather-bound object.

"Yes! Here it is!" he exclaims. He gives book to Teddy. Teddy peruses book's cover, slides right hand over slightly elevated image of school's eagle mascot perched atop carefully crafted letters and numbers.

"Oceanair 1977," Teddy reads. "A yearbook?"

"Do me a favor, pal," Principal Sims says. "Open that thing up and look at the table of contents. Find the page with the group photo of the graduating class for that year."

Teddy flips to page forty-nine, eyes smiling faces, beginning with furthest row back and ending with one in front. Attention rests upon image of boy with sepia skin and custom crafted shoes akin to his own.

"Calvin Cramer was his name," Principal Sims announces. "I believe this picture was taken one month after his dad returned from serving nine months on an aircraft carrier in the Indian Ocean. His dad's first tour of duty. He was in the Navy. While his dad was away during those nine months, Calvin's mom did her best to scrape by on the checks she received from his dad, but they were barely enough to keep food on the table, certainly not enough to splurge on new clothes and shoes. So, when Calvin began to outgrow his shoes, she cut them open to give her son some relief until they could afford new ones. She and Calvin made due with what they had. As you can see from the photo, Calvin, like the rest of his classmates, was a happy child, from all outward appearances anyway."

"Where's Calvin now?" Teddy asks.

"He's dead," Principal Sims replies. "Hung himself using bed sheets in the prison cell he shared with a man twice his age. If memory serves, I believe his cell mate had just left for the mess hall."

"Why'd he kill himself?" Teddy asks.

"Can anyone really know the demons that plague a person's mind?" Principal Sims asks, sighs. "Calvin's dad was a perfectionist and held himself, his wife, and his son to pretty high standards when it came to just about everything. In retrospect, one wonders what he would have done if he'd known his wife had cut holes in his son's shoes and sent him to school in them. I'm just assuming he didn't know, of course. But, I digress. Well, long after Calvin left Oceanair, his dad did his third extended tour of duty over in the Middle East. Calvin was in his late teens at that time and the economic situation was no different for him and his mother. So Calvin took it upon himself to do what he could to improve things."

"What did he do?" Teddy asks.

"Well, his deliveries started small, a few grams here or there to pick up some extra cash for him and his mom to make ends meet. Then, they got to be bigger and bigger. Calvin eventually became known as the king of his block in record time. He was known as the go-to guy for all the so-called 'good stuff' by the folks in his hood. Unfortunately for Calvin, he became a little too well known. An undercover cop eventually busted him. Rumor has it there was no way he would ever allow his dad to suffer the embarrassment of a son who sold, so...."

"No way," Teddy replies.

"Yep," Principal Sims says. "Again, this is just a rumor as to why he did it. Who knows where the truth lies?"

"Whoa," Teddy replies. "What a story!"

Principal Sims reclaims his seat.

"So, what's yours?" he asks.

"My what?" Teddy asks.

"Your story," Principal Sims says. He submerges left hand into back pants pocket, extracts heavily wrapped square, brick like object, weighing almost a pound. His pocket flattens immediately upon the object's removal. Principal Sims extends arm and hand towards Teddy.

"So, this fell from your pocket when I brought you to the office following your Tommy Hicks encounter."

"Oh, shit!" Teddy exclaims, nervously eyeing the package for signs of white powder remnants. None detected. Instinct compels hands to grip mouth briefly, then move slowly downward. "Um, sorry, sir."

"You don't have to apologize to me," Principal Sims says. He extends package and palm towards Teddy. "You want it back?"

Moisture wells in Teddy's eyes. Vision blurred, Teddy rotates frame away from Principal Sims and toward window affixed within the expanse of drywall farthest from office door. Torrents of rain buffet glass's exterior like stone pellets, the sound of each knocking on the door to Teddy's memory of the circumstance providing possible explanation for his present state. Door opens to fresh thoughts of last night's telephone conversation.

***

"Girl, I can't even begin to think about how I would come up with the rent for that place," Teddy's mother said. "It's $500 a month. As much as these people like me doin' their hair, ain't no way I can afford to open my own shop. Not with all I got going on right now. How am I gon' come up with $500 a month? I can't even buy new shoes for Teddy. And he growing so fast that earlier tonight night I had to cut...."

Teddy inclined his ear closer to his bedroom's threshold with hopes of identifying the familiar voice at other end of conversation. His mother's voice trailed off to a whisper.

"I know it's hard, baby sister," the woman replied.

Aha, Teddy thought. That's Aunt Polly. Thank goodness for speakerphone.

"But, keep the faith," Polly continued. "God's gon' make a way. By the way, I got some leftovers. Did y'all eat tonight?"

"I had a cup of cereal," Teddy's mother replied.

"And Teddy?" the woman asked.

"I brought him some leftover chicken from today's free lunch at the office. It's just so hard sometimes," Teddy's mother replied, amid stress-tinged tears.

"*You just hang in there,*" *Polly implored in hopes of keeping her sister's spirits up.* "*God's got it. Y'all gon' be all right.*"

* * *

A mother's dreams flattened by the anvil of responsibility, Teddy thinks. He cocks his head to the side, rejoins the present.

"I know it's tough, pal," Principal Sims says. He grips Teddy's shoulder. "And I know it's just you and your mom. But I want you to know you can always talk to me."

Teddy continues to stare outside, wipes wetness away from eyes, then turns.

"Yes, sir," Teddy replies.

Teddy accepts brick-like object from Principal Sims with right hand, moves away from window and toward office door.

"Hey, pal," Principal Sims says.

"Yep?" Teddy asks.

"I see you've got a free hand there. I know you're about to head off to class, but can you do me a favor and take a look at this when you have a few minutes?"

"What is it?" Teddy asks.

"It's just a flyer with some information about something I want you to think about."

"Okay," Teddy replies, accepts paper, begins to exit office.

"Wait, Teddy," Principal Sims says. "I've seen how funny you can be when you get around your friends. I mean, some of the stuff you come up with cracks me up. And your English teacher has told me about some of the stuff you've written in class—between you and me, she thinks you've really got a way with words."

"Me?" Teddy asks. "Yeah, right."

"I'm not pulling your leg, pal," Principal Sims replies. "Now, a comedy flash fiction competition is underway for students in your age group. And the deadline is the end of next week. Up to 500 words. Grand prize is $2000."

"Wow!" Teddy exclaims.

"Just think about it, Teddy," Principal Sims says. "The flyer has all the details."

"Yes, sir, I will," Teddy replies.

"Oh, one more thing," Principal Sims says.

"What's that?" Teddy asks.

"As principal of one of the co-sponsoring schools, I automatically get to be on the judging panel."

"Cool," Teddy replies.

"Now, I would have to think long and hard about being on that panel if one of my students actually enters the competition. Of course, I'd still have a say in who gets to take my place."

Teddy smiles. Exits office.

* * *

School bell rings, hastening the release of throngs of prepubescent pupils. They spill onto sun-soaked sidewalks and go their separate ways. Freedom. Until tomorrow. But, freedom, nonetheless.

Teddy lingers just inside school's main doors, peeks outside, spies Tommy Hicks and crew slither slowly down the road en route to offer coins to the arcade gods two blocks away.

I can't believe he didn't get expelled! Teddy thinks. *No justice, no peace! Well, at least the coast is clear.*

Teddy shoves mound of books into backpack, zips, then dips still open-toed shoes onto makeshift concrete catwalk fronting school. He struts along sidewalk slowly, glances down at recently gifted granddad's watch, one of few treasures inherited by his mom, now possessed by him.

2:30, it reads.

One hour left to deliver the package, Teddy thinks.

He inserts hand into pocket to confirm the presence of brick-shaped wad, sighs, then continues his stride past nearby elementary school. He pauses to witness neighborhood children frolicking across grass-free, dirt-ridden field, kicking soccer balls, jumping rope, tossing footballs. He wonders what stories lurk behind their smiles as they dart to-and-fro. He overhears group of boys' nascent, inexperienced efforts at playing the dozens.

"Yo mama so fat, she walk like 'dis," one boy says, then duck walks ten feet, belly thrust forward. Laughter ensues.

Teddy smiles. He shifts his gaze to two girls, perched in corner, sitting across from each other with legs crossed Indian style. Fists rise up, swoop down in rhythm quickly three times to meet palms.

Scissors, paper, rock. First girl displays scissor formation, second displays paper.

"Scissors cut paper!" first girl exclaims. "I win!"

Scissors, paper, rock. Second girl displays rock formation, first girl displays scissors.

"Rock crushes scissors!" second girl yells. "I win!"

Scissors, paper, rock. Second girl displays paper formation, first girl displays rock.

"Paper covers rock!" second girl exclaims. "I win again!"
Teddy smiles.

Paper covers rock, he thinks.

Teddy resumes street stride, gaining confidence with each step.

Paper covers rock, he thinks.

He pauses, extracts heavily wrapped wad from left pocket, removes backpack. He sits on bus stop bench, shifting his weight to the side. He takes paper out of his other pants pocket, unfolds it, reads.

GRAND PRIZE - $2000

He flips paper over, lays it atop heavily wrapped wad. He removes pencil from backpack.

Nerds and cool cats. Bookworms and hustlers. Circumstances and choices.

Now, what did I say to Hicks earlier today? Teddy thinks.

Teddy searches his memory. He looks down at his custom-made shoes. He smiles. He writes.

THE WORST

A human being being human. That's all it really amounted to. With all the fallibility that comes with it. Who could have predicted one lapse in judgment, one mistake, would lead to the spectacular downfall of one of the most respected talking heads in cable news? A reputation in tatters, consigned to the dustbin of history. A name that would carry with it an asterisk, one whose very mention in casual conversation would be forever followed by headshakes of pity or comments like "what a waste." And by the same human beings who, more likely than not, when left to their own devices (and web pages), probably engaged in far worse behavior than he behind closed doors. The only distinction being the absence of a camera to capture and broadcast their activities to the masses.

Nevertheless, the unspoken pact not to bring embarrassment and shame upon the pantheon of cable news had been broken. So, on that cloudy September afternoon—a mere fifty minutes after the video footage snaked its way around the world wide web, Vidal Gopol was handed his walking papers and given less than two hours to pack his things and leave.

On the train ride home, he made a halfhearted attempt to shield himself from the glares and whispers from onlookers who were not accustomed to being in the presence of disgraced television news royalty. His dark tinted sunglasses and raised newspaper were ineffective in that effort. His inability to endure the tsunami of judgment bearing down on him prompted an earlier than planned exit from the rail car. A cacophony of rancid odors greeted him when he ascended the subway's escalators and reached street level. Reflex compelled his right hand to cup his nostrils to protect him from the pungent onslaught. A few feet away, he spied the tail end of a line of bodies that hugged the buildings anchoring the sidewalk.

It led to a strangely familiar and well-aged edifice at the end of the street. Curiosity coaxed his feet to follow the line to its ultimate destination. He strode the length of the line, careful to keep his distance from the dirt-ridden bodies that appeared not to have been washed in months. A ten-foot door framed by an archway accented by gold spackled paint separated those at the front of the line from whatever awaited them on the other side. Vidal eyed the paint chips that flaked and hung precariously from the upper regions of the archway above him. The latch to the door released with a loud crack causing some of the flakes to fall. The door swung back and a brown-skinned elderly woman stepped forward.

"Ready for the next ten, please," she said.

Vidal observed ten bodies at the front of the line step past the door's threshold and enter the building as the woman counted each one of them. When she finished counting, she noticed Vidal staring at her. She lowered her wire-framed glasses and locked eyes with him.

"My word," she began. "I can't believe it. Vidal Gopol, is that you?"

"Excuse me?" Vidal replied.

"My little helper," the woman said. "It *is* you. I could recognize that unruly curly mop of hair anywhere."

She enveloped him in an instant.

"Now, you come inside right now so I can get a good look at you," she said. "It's been ages."

"You know me?" Vidal asked.

"Do I *know* you?" the woman replied. "I know you, all right. And not from that disloyal network you work for, or should I say 'worked' for. I've known you since you were this high."

She folded her body slightly and moved her right hand to her kneecaps.

"Really?" Vidal asked. "Because I don't recognize you at all. Though I have to say there's something very familiar about this place."

"I bet there is," the woman replied, smiling. "After all, you used to come here with your parents, God rest their souls, from the time you could walk. Your mother used to help us in the kitchen, while your father would roll out the cots for us. You, on the other hand, would always sit patiently in that corner right over there—always with your nose in some book. Except for one day, and only one day. When I was able to convince you to help me paint that archway out there. You did a really good job too. Only recently has the paint started to crack. Was bound to happen over time, I guess. Nothing really lasts forever."

"It's crazy that I don't remember any of that, Miss....," Vidal began.

"Ashkar," the woman said. "Aperna Ashkar."

"So, the people you serve here, I take it they are homeless?"

"That they are, Vidal," Ms. Ashkar replied. "But that's just one thing they are. Some of them are mentally ill, others have been poor their whole lives and still others are highly intelligent, multi-degreed professionals who, by virtue of circumstance, just happen to find themselves at our doorstep in need of a little help. For an afternoon, or a night or several nights."

"And my parents?" Vidal asked. "I don't remember too much about them, I'm ashamed to say. My adoptive parents didn't allow me to keep very much from my life before. I think they wanted to protect me from having to re-live the trauma of their deaths from the car accident."

"Your birth parents, Vidal," Ms. Ashkar began. "Fell into the latter category. Highly respected professionals in their fields of chemistry and medicine who volunteered their time religiously—at least three times a week."

"Really?" Vidal asked.

"Yes, they did," Ms. Ashkar replied. "They very much subscribed to the belief that for whom much is given, much is required because they knew that but before the grace of God...."

"I see," Vidal said.

"It is so good to see you, Vidal, after all these years," Ms. Ashkar said. "But, if you will excuse me, I *do* need to head to the kitchen to assist with the serving. You, of course, are welcome to stay as long as you like. You are back home, after all."

She squeezed Vidal's hand, locked eyes with him and smiled before disappearing behind a large door across the room. Vidal lifted his frame from the chair in which he sat. He made his way out of the room and down the well-lit corridor adjacent to it. Its walls were adorned with framed photos of people Vidal presumed had assisted in the facility's efforts over the years. Vidal continued to survey the photos until one of a striking Indian couple with a curly-haired boy nestled between them came into view. Vidal removed his glasses, inclined his head toward the picture to get a closer look. He wiped moisture from the corners of his eyes at the sight of his parents before continuing his journey down the length of the corridor. He opened the door at the end of the hall. When he did so, a booming baritone voice barreled towards him when he entered the kitchen. The man shouted as if he were announcing the commencement of the best show on Earth.

> *Come one, come all! Step right up and get your free lunch here! Come as you are, no judgment here! No money, no nothing required! Just step right up! We'll take care of you real good!*

Aperna Ashkar patted the man on the back as the center's patrons looked on. She embraced him as laughter overtook them both. She spied Vidal in the doorway and gave him a reassuring nod. He stepped past the trays and utensils toward the rear of the kitchen where an apron, hair net and pair of plastic gloves awaited him. He put them on and turned towards Aperna Ashkar.

"Where do I go from here?" he asked.

PRIVILEGE

ANY LITTLE EXTRA

The elegantly attired brunette swept wayward wisps of hair behind her ear with the freshly manicured tip of her right index finger at the moment her left hand rendezvoused with her husband's in the middle of the table. He rested his free hand atop the platinum credit card he'd laid on the bill the Jamaican-American waitress stealthily deposited moments earlier during her most recent visit to the couple.

"Let's leave cash tonight, darling," the woman said. "Remember, she won't get the full amount of her tip if you use the card."

"You're right, dear," her husband replied. "And the service here certainly was exceptional tonight, wasn't it?"

The woman nodded and smiled in agreement.

"How about this?" her husband began. "What if I put dinner on the card, but then leave the tip in cash? That way she—what's her name, Pamela?"

"I believe so, yes, darling."

"That way Pamela gets the full amount of her tip and I still get some points for using my card out of this deal!"

"Fine," the woman replied. "After all, we can never have *too* many points… which we never really use!"

She waved the white cloth napkin with the small green, black, and yellow embossed banner in its corner for effect.

Stephanie and Tanner Lancaster stared at each other briefly, then chuckled. An inadvertent finger graze across the small circular button at the bottom of Stephanie Lancaster's smartphone brought the device to life.

"My word, Tanner," she said. "Look at the time. We need to leave soon. I want to be sure to get home in enough time to review Megan's personal statement and résumé one last time before she goes to bed. Remember, the Ivy reps will be at the college fair tomorrow."

"Oh, that's right!" Tanner Lancaster exclaimed. "I'd forgotten about that. Big day tomorrow!"

He signaled for the waitress to collect his card and the bill.

"Sure is, darling," Stephanie Lancaster replied. "I know you've got your legacy connections and the tutor we hired to get her through the entrance exam also helped. But it's so competitive these days, what with all 'the others' they let in for the sake of so-called 'inclusion.' So, any little extra we can do will help."

"You're so right, dear," Tanner Lancaster said. "As usual."

"Well, I sure hope you enjoyed yourselves this evening and that everything was prepared to your liking," the waitress said. She reached for the still-cold bottle of sparkling water to refill the couple's glasses one last time with her right hand, while collecting the bill and credit card with her left.

"Everything was great, sweetheart," Stephanie Lancaster replied. "And, let me just say, you have been simply wonderful!"

"Well, thank you so much," the waitress replied. "It's been a pleasure serving you both. We sure hope you come back to visit us soon."

"We certainly will," Stephanie Lancaster said.

She inclined her head towards the waitress and cupped her hands around her lips as if she were about to convey a secret she did not want the other diners to hear.

She whispered, "We loved the food. We are just so happy you all opened earlier this year. It's been years since we've had any quality ethnic cuisine in the area. Please give our regards to the owner—Clive, is it?"

"Yes, it is, ma'am," the waitress replied.

"Oh, I figured based on the restaurant's name," Stephanie Lancaster said, noting the impressively embossed "*C*" on the menu resting in the cradle of the waitress's left arm. "Well, please give him and the chef our regards. Everything was excellent."

"I'll definitely do that, ma'am," the waitress replied. "I'll be right back with this so you can sign."

She turned to commence her trek towards the cashier.

"Oh wait," Tanner Lancaster began. The waitress paused. He sank his hand into his pocket and removed two twenty-dollar bills. He extended them towards the waitress. "I almost forgot. This is for you."

"Oh, thank you, sir," the waitress replied. "That is so kind."

"No, we should be thanking you," Tanner Lancaster said. "As my wife said, you were just wonderful tonight."

"That's sweet of you both to say," the waitress replied. "Thank you again. It's been my pleasure—really."

She turned to leave.

"Oh, I'm sorry," Tanner Lancaster said. "One more thing. Would you be a dear and take this to the valet while you're at it? We're in a hurry to get home and if it's not too much of an imposition, we'd really appreciate it."

The waitress accepted the yellow valet slip while attempting to maintain her smile as the twinkle in eye her began to fade.

"Of course, sir," she said. "I'll be right back."

"She sure is a sweetheart," Stephanie Lancaster said.

"Isn't she?" Tanner Lancaster replied.

The couple lifted their glasses and pushed them gently towards each other until they met before taking final sips.

***

"How much longer do you think before we can go home, babe?" Pamela Mitchell asked. She wiped down the final three tables in the dining room before refilling small bottles of Scotch Bonnet pepper sauce to place at the center of each one.

"I'd say another thirty minutes at least," Clive Mitchell replied. "I know these days it is considered un-American to require people to pay with cash, but almost everyone in this country uses credit cards, man. And you know what that means."

"What?" Pamela Mitchell asked.

"It means a percentage discount off our money. And you know we've got rent and overhead and I promised the staff I'd give them a little something extra for all the late nights during these first few months."

"I know you did, babe," Pamela Mitchell said. "Well, for what it's worth, almost all my customers said they loved the food and told me they will be coming back, so that's good news, right?"

"Good news, yes," Clive Mitchell replied. "But we'll see how long they will continue to come after I raise prices, which is looking like a very real possibility if things keep going at this rate. I know it's a rare thing to make any real money during the first year of opening, but I'm beginning to think it's doubtful that we can break even!"

"Well, let's see how things look at the end of the month before making any decisions about prices," Pamela Mitchell said. "In the meantime, if you need money for the staff, I'll contribute too. After all, I've been making a good amount of cash in tips this week. I just need to make sure I keep at least twenty dollars because Paulina will need it for tomorrow."

"Oh, that's right!" Clive Mitchell replied. "I forgot all about tomorrow. She texted me good night earlier and I didn't even have time to call to wish her good luck because of how busy it got."

"Busy is a blessing, babe," Pamela Mitchell said. "And your daughter understands. I called her briefly during my early break. She was able to warm the dinner I left for her before I came to help you get ready for the dinner rush. And I reminded her she needs to turn in early tonight to make sure she gets a full night's rest."

"I'm sure she's in bed by now, so no need to call, huh?" Clive Mitchell asked.

"Babe, don't beat yourself up about this," Pamela Mitchell replied. "She's good. She understands what you're trying to build here and appreciates that. It's one of the main reasons—and I know this will make you smile—she told me she wants to be a business major when she goes to college next year."

"Yes, I like the sound of that," Clive Mitchell said. "A business major *'when'* she goes to college. Because she's definitely going. Even if I have to sell my right arm! Babe, wouldn't it be great if she got into the best of the best?"

"Yes, it would," Pamela Mitchell replied. "You know her grades have always been stellar. That, coupled with her entrance exam score and extracurriculars, makes me think it might be a real possibility."

"Yes," Clive Mitchell said. "She knocked it out of the park on that entrance exam, didn't she? And on the first try!"

"Yes, our baby did," Pamela Mitchell replied. "And thank God she did because I don't know how we would have gotten the money for her to take that test again."

"That's for sure," Clive Mitchell said. "But, speaking of money, if she does get in one of the elites, the ball will be back in our court, babe. We'll pray for the scholarships, but if not...."

"If not...," Pamela Mitchell replied.

They both sighed.

"Let's cross that bridge when we get to it," Clive Mitchell said. "In the meantime, how much did you say you made from your tips?"

"Here you go, babe," Pamela Mitchell replied.

She pushed a wad of cash towards him.

"And, when is that food critic supposed to be stopping by?" Clive Mitchell asked. "The online comments have been great, but we sure could use some good *official* press these days too."

"That's a good question," Pamela Mitchell replied. "Give me a minute. Let me go grab my phone. I'm pretty sure I put the date in my calendar."

* * *

Megan Lancaster glanced at the screen of her smartphone and noted the time as perspiration began to pool beneath the blonde bangs that sheltered her forehead.

"C'mon, c'mon," she whispered to herself.

She turned to her right to gaze worriedly through the window of the private coach her parents had rented to shepherd the group of sixty seniors to the premier college recruiters fair in the Northeast. Her mind raced with speculation on what unfortunate circumstance could explain why her friend had yet to make an appearance.

"Is this seat taken?" the red-headed jock asked as he made his way down the center aisle.

"Yes," Megan Lancaster snapped without hesitation. "It's saved."

She placed her designer handbag in the seat next to her to discourage any future queries on the matter. She turned back towards the window and moved the strands of hair that had begun to obstruct her view behind her right ear so she could continue to search for her friend. She surveyed the sea of students that moved on the opposite side of the window for a full minute without sensing the presence of the mocha hued hand lifting her handbag. The purse landed in Megan's lap with a thud.

"What's his name?" Paulina Mitchell asked.

She folded herself into the leather-bound seat that had been reserved for her.

"Whose name?" Megan Lancaster asked.

"Whoever it is that's got your attention outside that window right now," Paulina Mitchell replied.

"If you *must* know, I was looking for you," Megan Lancaster said. "What took you so long?"

She swatted her friend on the arm.

"Ouch!" Paulina Mitchell replied. "Girl, the bus was late picking me up this morning. You know it takes me almost an hour to get from my house to school on a *good* day."

Megan stared blankly at her friend.

"Well, today was *not* a good day," Paulina Mitchell continued. "What time did you get here?"

"My mom dropped me off about thirty minutes ago," Megan Lancaster replied. "With enough time to go grab a coffee. It's my second cup of the day, by the way. Not as good as the one I had earlier, I'll say."

She grabbed and raised the paper cup from the tray table in front of her. Paulina Mitchell rolled her eyes.

"My nanny had my first cup waiting for me in the kitchen as soon as Alexa woke me up," Megan Lancaster continued. "It was delish. This is not nearly as good by comparison, but it'll do. I figure I need to do whatever I can to be extra alert today. Want some?"

She extended the coffee towards her friend.

"Um, no," Paulina Mitchell replied. "I'm good."

"Okay, then," Megan Lancaster said. "More for me. By the way, how you feeling about all this?"

"I'm fine I guess," Paulina Mitchell replied.

"Well, of course you are," Megan Lancaster said. "You're always so cool, calm, and collected. And with your grades and your entrance exam score, I know you're going to crush it! Me, on the other hand...."

"You'll be fine, Megan," Paulina Mitchell replied.

"I hope so," Megan Lancaster said. "We'll see. I'm just glad you made it in time. Looks like we're going to push off in less than five."

***

Glossy hard copy brochures competed for attention with electronic tablets, laptops and Smart TV screens, all of which beckoned onlookers to behold the benefits of attending the myriad of institutions of higher learning on display. Paulina Mitchell and Megan Lancaster weaved their way through the throngs of students, past the second and third tier schools en route to the convention center's inner sanctum, which had been reserved for the first-tier schools and the Ivy's. It was separated from the masses by a velvet rope, two smartly attired table attendants and a security guard.

"Girl, you won't believe this, but I need to run to the ladies' room before heading in there," Paulina Mitchell said.

"Oh, okay," Megan Lancaster replied. "How funny is it that I drank all the coffee this morning and here you are needing to go to the potty?"

"Nerves, girl," Paulina Mitchell said. "I'm not so cool, calm, and collected after all, I guess."

"Well, imagine that," Megan Lancaster began. "You're human!"

Paulina Mitchell swatted her friend on the arm.

"Ouch!" Megan Lancaster laughed. "That hurt."

"Well, you hit me earlier," Paulina Mitchell replied, laughing. "That's payback! Anyway, I gotta go."

"Go ahead," Megan Lancaster said. "I'll wait for you."

"Don't be silly, girl. Go on in and I'll meet you inside."

"Well, all right," Megan replied. "I'll see you inside."

Paulina Mitchell turned towards the ladies' room, while Megan Lancaster continued towards the velvet rope.

"Twenty dollars, please," the rosy-cheeked table attendant said.

"Excuse me?" Megan Lancaster replied. "I paid my twenty when I entered the convention center. Are you telling me it's an additional twenty to get into this section?"

"Yes, sweetie," the table attendant said.

"Well, they didn't tell us that," Megan Lancaster replied. "Well, okay. I don't have cash, but...."

She reached down into her handbag to remove one of her credit cards as the line behind her began to swell.

"Just give me a minute," Megan Lancaster said.

"Megan, is that you?"

Megan Lancaster shifted her focus from her handbag to the high-pitched voice that spoke her name. She turned to her left to catch a glimpse of the well-dressed New Englander that had begun to sashay towards her. Megan

Lancaster stared blankly as the woman's varicose-veined claws encircled Megan and pulled her in.

"It's me," the woman said. "Veronica Wilmington. You remember me, don't you? I'm a friend of your mama."

"Oh, hi!" Megan replied.

"Remember, I helped run the debutante ball two years ago!"

"Oh, yes, that's right," Megan replied.

"You were by far the prettiest one to turn out that year," the woman said. "And look at you now! Still as pretty as a daisy."

"Why, thank you," Megan Lancaster replied.

"Are you getting ready to go into the 'VIP Suite' as we affectionately call it?" the woman asked.

"Yes," Megan replied. "But I didn't know it was an additional twenty dollars to get in there, so I just need to give them my credit—"

"Don't be silly," the woman interrupted. "I'm in charge here."

She removed a gold-ribboned badge from her suit jacket and shoved it towards the rosy-cheeked table attendant.

"You just go right on in," she said.

The table attendant unhooked and moved the velvet rope to the side to permit Megan Lancaster entry. Ten minutes elapsed before Paulina Mitchell found herself at the front of the line.

"Your credentials, please," the rosy-cheeked table attendant said.

"Oh, right," Paulina Mitchell replied. She lifted her ID badge and turned it around so the table attendant could confirm her name, grade point average and entrance exam score.

"Twenty dollars, please."

"Excuse me?" Paulina Mitchell said. "I already spent twenty to get into this fair earlier. Are you telling me it costs another twenty to get into this section?"

"Yes, ma'am," the table attendant replied. "It's an additional twenty."

"Well, no one told me that," Paulina Mitchell said. "I don't have another twenty dollars."

"Well, there's a cash machine on the far side of the room over there," the table attendant replied. "Or, you can just use your card here."

"I don't have a card," Paulina Mitchell replied. "I only had the twenty."

"Well, I'm sorry, ma'am," the table attendant said. "Is there someone you can call to bring you the money or do you have someone here who can loan it to you?"

Paulina Mitchell looked past the velvet rope to see her friend in the distance chatting excitedly with a recruiter from one of the elites. Then, she looked down at her smartphone. She thought of her parents who'd been sleeping when she left the house before sunrise. She knew they likely were in full preparation mode for the restaurant's lunch rush. She turned to look at the long line of students behind her and smiled.

"No," Paulina Mitchell said. "But thanks for your help."

She moved out of the line to make way for the other students, turned around and began to weave her way back through the throng of humanity from which she'd emerged to find some glossy hard copy brochures, electronic tablets, and Smart TV screens to occupy her time.

SELF-EVIDENT TRUTHS

"True dat!" Aaron exclaimed. He adjusted the cell phone that had been glued to his ear for the better part of ten minutes, then moved his hand down and cupped it, the perfect receptacle for the diamonds that fell from his other pale palm like a miniature waterfall.

He hated to admit when his best friend was right. But, on this issue, he had no choice. The jewelry he and Ken lifted tonight had been the best score they'd made in the past three years. Of course, Aaron didn't *need* the gems. For him, the burglaries were a recreational activity, engaged in purely for the thrill and fun of it. Although one couldn't tell it from his current b-boy appearance, Aaron had grown up with the best. The son of a United States Senator worth millions before he was even born, Aaron's pathway to the finer things in life had almost been preordained.

Ken, by contrast, despite the clean-cut image he projected as he crashed one upscale party after the next with the designer suits and watches he'd stolen during his five-year swing through South Florida with Aaron, had grown up the son of a poverty-stricken, high-cheekboned, blonde haired, blue eyed drug addict. *Po white trash* was the term his so-called friends used to describe his mother when he was a child. The phrase the neighborhood kids had hurled his way while he was growing up was permanently engrained into his psyche like a tattoo.

Ken rationalized his stealing by thinking that he embodied the person of a modern-day Robin Hood. So what if the so-called riches he amassed had not been shared with his mother who had done everything she could to clean herself up but, somehow, always managed to fall short. No amount of cash he accumulated could have straightened the doomed path on which she was destined to travel, Ken thought. So, instead of funding her stay at the rehab facility Aaron told him about years earlier, Ken funded his new wardrobe and fueled his lavish lifestyle. *It would be money thrown down the drain* was Ken's response when Aaron initially raised the issue. Wasn't the fact that Ken used the money he stole to fund his own transition from poverty to privilege enough of a fulfillment of Hood's mission? Well, it would have to be, Aaron thought.

* * *

A single tear slid down Sasha Freemont's cheek and chin to connect with the face linked to the body that lay less than three feet beneath her. She smiled as the droplet slid from the caramel-colored cadaver's lifeless skin until it was

absorbed into the gray garment that was still attached to its head.
"He always liked hoodies," she said to the detective that stood next to the body.

"I think I already know the answer but, ma'am, do you recognize this individual?" the detective asked, noting the unmistakable resemblance between the face of the corpse and that of the mocha-colored beauty that stood before him.

At this question, Sasha could contain the fullness of her grief no longer. Tears spewed from her eyes as if from a volcano. She unsuccessfully attempted to push back behind her ears the braids that escaped the scrunchy she had carefully assembled hours before while looking at herself in the mirror in preparation for the possibility of this moment. Then, she spoke.

"This is my son."

"I'm sorry, ma'am," the detective replied.

"Can you tell me where you found him?" Sasha asked.

"He was found facedown in an open grassy area in the Brookmeade subdivision about five miles East of Sanford, Florida, ma'am."

"And how did he...?" she began to ask, fighting back tears.

"A gunshot, ma'am," the detective replied.

"Where?" she asked.

"Through the chest."

"Okay," she said. "Okay."

The smile that had disappeared minutes earlier when she was asked to identify her son reappeared briefly as Sasha noticed the startled, frozen expression that was now permanently displayed on her son's face, the same expression she recalled him exhibiting the day she found him after the fire that almost took his father's life. Her son had been a hero that day, running into the room from which the smoke billowed as his dad lay unconscious and helpless next to his bed. How her son had managed to summon the physical strength necessary to lift and drag a man almost three times his size to safety remained a mystery to Sasha.

The look on his face, the same one she saw now, signaled that perhaps it had been just as much a mystery to her son. All Sasha knew was that her fourteen-year-old boy, no—her little man—had done this. And, after first scolding him for being so foolish as to put himself in harm's way, she had to admit to herself that she had been proud of him. For as long as she could remember, her son frequently exhibited qualities that made it perfectly understandable how he could place the life of someone else before his own. She had envisioned a career in law enforcement for him. His father, by contrast, after the incident, wanted nothing of it. He preferred seeing his son working in the safe confines of an office. How could it be that just a mere three years later her son lay here lifeless, unable to fulfill the dreams either of them had for him? Tears revisited her.

"Ma'am, I'm sorry that you have to go through this, but I do need to ask you a few more questions."

"Okay," Sasha replied.

"I know his name because I found it inscribed on his license when he pulled his wallet and a bag of candy from his pockets," the detective said. "The license was stuck next to the emergency contact card with your and your husband's names and phone numbers. Great idea to have him carry that with him, ma'am."

"Ex-husband," Sasha said.

"Excuse me, ma'am?"

"His father is my ex-husband," Sasha replied.

"My apologies, ma'am. The card with your ex-husband's name and number," the detective replied. "As I said, we found his name when we removed the wallet and license from his pocket, but we are still unclear what your son was doing in the neighborhood. Can you shed any light on that for us?"

"Of course, I can," Sasha replied, as she waged a losing battle against her tears. "He was visiting his father and his father's new girlfriend. They just moved to Brookmeade a couple of months ago. It was his dad's visitation weekend."

"My question is how is it that a young man who was walking in his father's neighborhood could suddenly be shot dead? Can you shed some light on that for me?"

"Well, we're trying to get to the bottom of that, ma'am," the detective replied. "And the information you're giving me now is going a long way to help us do just that."

When the detective concluded his statement, Sasha could not help but be distracted by the image of the man standing on the other side of the glass in the adjacent room as he rubbed what appeared to be blood from the back of his bald head. The handkerchief he used to do so looked eerily familiar to her. When she saw the *TM* stitching in the bottom left-hand corner of the cloth, she stood and pointed.

"Why is that man using my son's handkerchief to wipe his head?"

"What handkerchief?" the detective asked.

"That handkerchief," Sasha said. She pointed again in the bald man's direction. The officer unfolded himself from the chair in which he'd been sitting and moved quickly to close the blinds that covered the glass separating the morgue from the room that housed the bald man.

"I can't get into that right now with you, ma'am," the detective said. "Let's stay focused."

"Stay focused?" Sasha replied. "I *am* focused. I'm focused on the monogrammed handkerchief I gave my son when he turned fourteen, just a month before he saved his dad from a burning fire. And I'm wondering why that man has it in his hand."

"Ma'am, please, let's just stay—" the detective began.

"No, I want to know why!" Sasha exclaimed. She stood up and began to walk quickly toward the door connecting the two rooms.

The detective swiftly advanced to restrain Sasha, intercepting her before she reached the door. "Okay, ma'am. I'll tell you."

"Okay," Sasha said.

"That is the man who found your son."

* * *

Garry Zeller replayed in his mind over and again the events that had transpired three hours earlier that evening, as he continued to wipe the remaining blood from the back of his head.

"Why didn't I just stay in the car?" he whispered to himself.

"I'm sorry, sir?" Officer Krantz asked. "Did you just say something?"

"Um, no," Zeller replied. "I'm just clearing my throat."

* * *

Zeller had always prided himself on getting it right. But how could he have been so wrong this time? From what he could see, the kid was wearing baggy jeans that hung below his waist, he strolled through the grass with that gangster walk they like to do, and he had that gray hood draped over his head like he was hiding something. Sure, it had been raining earlier. But what other reason could the kid have for wearing that hood and being in Garry's neighborhood if not to rob someone or cause some kind of trouble?

Between the hours of eight and midnight. Those were the prime hours when the robbers had struck in the past. Why should tonight have been any different? And the kid was the only one he saw in the area—with the exception of the two college aged kids with polos and khakis who were heading in the opposite direction out of the neighborhood. Though he'd never seen them before, he was certain they probably were relatives of one of the families in the subdivision, perhaps home for break. After the rash of burglaries in the area, Garry had been tired of others talking about doing more to protect the neighborhood.

He had decided he was going to take it upon himself to act. And he did not recall any neighbor raising one objection to that at the last homeowner's association meeting. So, he acted. At the time, it did not matter that the 9-1-1 dispatcher had said not to follow the kid when he called. Waiting for the police would have given the kid more than enough time to do the deed and leave.

When he approached the kid and asked him what he was doing in the neighborhood, he thought he saw him—no, he was sure he saw him—reach down to grab a weapon. Startled by the move and not realizing the grass beneath him was still wet from the rain, Garry recalled losing his footing as he stepped back and reached down for his gun. In what seemed like a millisecond, the back of Garry's head made contact with the concrete sidewalk that abutted the blades of grass on which he had been standing. He had been thankful that the fall had not caused him to black out completely because he somehow managed with both hands to keep the barrel of his gun aimed directly at the kid's chest.

"Drop your weapon!" Garry exclaimed, as he removed his left hand from the gun to steer it toward the back of his head where a pool of blood had begun to form.

"What weapon?" the kid replied. "I don't have a weapon."

"Yes, you do," Garry said.

"Help! Help!" the kid began to scream.

"Shut up," Garry replied, in a loud whisper.

"Help!" the kid continued.

"I said shut the fuck up!" Garry shouted in a voice louder than the kid's, but not so loud as to overtake the thunderous sound of the bullet's escape form the barrel of the gun. Then, silence.

* * *

"Mr. Zeller," Officer Krantz said. He snapped his finger in front of Garry's face in an effort to awaken Garry from his apparent trance.

"So, you were saying the kid grabbed you and threw you to the ground. And that's how you got the injury on the back of your head?"

"Um, yes," Garry replied. "He threw me to the ground and started slamming my head to the ground. And that's when I shot him."

"And the handkerchief, sir?" Officer Krantz asked. "Where did that come from?"

"I, uh," Garry began. He gazed down at the monogrammed handkerchief he had removed from the kid's pocket when he had earlier searched for a gun.

* * *

"Dude, I'm just glad we got out of there when we did," Ken said. He adjusted the cell phone from the left side of his head to the right with one hand, while lifting the flute of champagne from the room service tray he previously ordered with the other. It had become a ritual of sorts for him and Aaron to cap off a successful heist by each checking separately into swanky, preferably five-star, hotels so they could begin to enjoy the fruits of their labor and celebrate.

"True dat," Aaron replied, while maneuvering behind his ear one of the blond locks that had fallen over his cheek. "A mo' fucking gunshot, yo. I know dat's what it was."

"Wonder if that creepy cracker that was checking us out before he started following that kid in the hoodie was involved," Ken said.

"Dude, let's not even think about dat right now," Aaron replied. "Whatever happened, remember, we didn't see shit. And we don't know shit."

"Yep. By the way, dawg, I know you like your b-boy style, but I think you made a good call on the khakis and polos tonight. If anybody's got surveillance cameras up in that joint, they will never suspect it was us," Ken laughed.

Ken then reached past the stack of cash he and Aaron took from the three story mini-mansion in Brookmeade earlier, grabbed the remote resting atop his minibar, pressed the Power button and stared openmouthed at the on-screen footage of the blood stain on the sidewalk he and Aaron had walked down a few hours earlier. He adjusted the volume just as the reporter spoke.

**

"This is the scene at 5563 Tranquil Lane in the Brookmeade subdivision just East of Sanford, Florida," the reporter said. "As you can see, the police have cordoned off this area completely with crime scene tape as they investigate. Details at this stage are sketchy, but preliminary reports indicate that a gunshot was heard by multiple residents at approximately 9:30 p.m. this evening. There also were reports of shouting prior to the gunshot. I believe I see someone who looks like she may be a resident approaching now. Let me see if I can... ma'am, ma'am. How are you, ma'am? We are reporting live for WKVR-TV. Can you tell us anything about what you observed this evening?"

"Well, I did hear a gunshot," the woman replied. She moved recently dyed coal-colored bangs across her pale, surgically tightened forehead. "Just as I was unpacking the groceries from my car. And I know we have been having a lot of robberies lately. I don't know if the shot had anything to do with that at all. Aside from that, I don't know anything else really."

"Thanks, ma'am," the reporter said. "We appreciate your time. And, so that's the scene at this hour in the upscale subdivision of Brookmeade. Wait, I'm being passed a piece of paper as I speak. Apparently, we also know that a body has been recovered and the police do have a man in custody. We will keep you updated as additional details become available. Until then, I'm—"

"I'm sorry," the woman interrupted. "There was something else I forgot to mention."

"What's that, ma'am?" the reporter asked.

"I do recall seeing a young black man walking down the street as I turned into my drive way," the woman replied. "A young black man wearing baggy pants and a gray jacket with a hood on it, I believe. Yes, a suspicious-looking young man. I saw that too."

"Thank you, ma'am," the reporter said.

* * *

"Dude, are you still on the phone?" Aaron asked. "Earth to Ken."

"Oh, yeah," Ken replied, while directing his focus back to the phone conversation.

"Where did you go just now?" Aaron asked. "And what were we talking about?"

"Khakis and polos, yo," Ken replied. "Nothing but khakis and polos from here on out."

"Yeah, okay, okay!" Aaron exclaimed. "You said dat shit already. I got it." He eyed his pale fingers as they lay atop the gems that were spread across his bed.

"Dude, I'm as white as these diamonds. I need to get a tan."

"No, you don't, dawg," Ken said, still eyeing the BREAKING NEWS caption on the television screen. "Trust me. No. You. Don't. Turn on the TV."

Aaron reached for the remote as Ken said this and, seconds later, became immediately transfixed by the BREAKING NEWS caption and the description of the night's events, which now included the resident's observations, that scrolled beneath it.

"True dat!" Aaron said, as he divided his attention between the gems on his bed and the words on the screen.

SMALL TALK

Seamlessly shifting among topics about which one knows little while balancing beverage, preferably alcoholic, in non-handshake hand.
    A skill conspicuously absent from the qualifications section of the job posting. And a formidable, though not insurmountable, challenge at the firm's first summer social gathering for Malcolm Reid, rising third-year law student who'd bested several equally qualified candidates for one of eight coveted law clerk positions. He'd not formally prepared to navigate this very important aspect of what he rightly realized amounted to an extended job interview masquerading as a dinner party. But he was ready. Whether he realized it or not, his years of observation under the tutelage of his astute, quick-thinking father in similar settings had prepared him well.
    Malcolm smiled briefly, patiently awaiting the bartender's final garnishment of his cocktail glass. He recalled how much he dreaded being dragged from one banquet to the next as a child to witness his dad receive one award after another, wishing instead he could simply spend his time shooting hoops with his friends. After his mother succumbed to recurring bouts of pancreatic cancer, his relationship with his father had somehow morphed during his middle school years from that of dutiful son to caretaker, to frequent dinner companion. He did not have a sibling with whom to share the responsibility. It was his alone. So, as he stood at his father's elbow all those years ago with soft drink in hand, he simply listened, observed and, while he may not have been really conscious of it at the time, learned.

* * *

"There you go again, Lieutenant, showing up all the competition," Admiral Boone began. "What's this now? Your fourth award in the past two months?"
    He slapped Malcolm's father on the back for emphasis, prompting laughter from Rear Admirals Tate and Reardon.
    "Well, you know, sir, it's a burden," Malcolm's dad had said. "But someone around here has to bite the bullet and give the next generation something to aspire to."
    He patted Malcolm on the head, causing his audience of three to smile.
    "Well said," Rear Admiral Tate replied.

* * *

Malcolm's dad had entered the Navy at nineteen. Though he'd never say so, it was more out of necessity than anything else. Malcolm knew his dad had been well on his way to pursuing his true passion of becoming a major league shortstop when he got an unexpected call from Malcolm's mother informing his dad that she was pregnant. They were married less than a month later. In those days, that's what many men did. It was a subject that was never discussed in the household while Malcolm was growing up, but it was one about which he'd become keenly aware when he was ten. He'd been searching for his baseball glove in the attic when he stumbled upon photos of his dad dressed smartly in his minor league baseball uniform alongside his other teammates.

The image sparked Malcolm's curiosity and prompted him to go directly to the source of each and every morsel of family lore Malcolm desired—his paternal grandfather. Never one to hold back information, upon inquiry, Malcolm's granddad fed Malcolm's curiosity with facts about all there was to know about his dad's decision to forego the less than guaranteed glory of major sports superstardom in exchange for marriage and the certainty of a career that would ensure he could provide for his burgeoning young family.

Malcolm had always questioned the closeness in time between his parents' wedding anniversary and his birthday. When he was old enough, he only had to do the math. But his granddad's commentary provided him the missing piece of a puzzle he'd been trying to solve his entire life to that point. And the revelation only made him admire his dad that much more.

* * *

"Well, I'll tell you," Rear Admiral Reardon began. "You certainly have given your boy something to aspire to. I mean, if I'd had a dad that reached the level you have as a role model, who knows where I'd be right now?"

Though not perceptible to the casual onlooker, Malcolm noted the way his dad's teeth clenched ever so slightly at these types of statements. He masked it well with his smile, but it was there.

"Well, I'm sure you did okay for yourself, sir," Malcolm's dad replied. "I'm convinced of that."

He raised his glass, consumed the alcohol inside, then crunched into multiple pieces the ice cube that hovered within.

"Well, thank you, Lieutenant," Rear Admiral Reardon replied. "That's mighty kind of you."

"Just stating the facts, sir," Malcolm's dad said.

"Well, now that you two have finished stroking each other's Johnsons, I have a question for you," Rear Admiral Tate said.

"What's that?" Rear Admiral Reardon asked.

"What do you all make of all this talk about information technology? I don't know about y'all, but all this news about bits and bytes makes my head spin. My wife tells me we should buy stock in that new startup computer company, what's it called—Micro-something—or another? But I just don't know. What say you, Lieutenant?"

"Well, I'll tell you," Malcolm's dad began. "The only 'byte' I'm familiar with is the one I almost got the other day when our next-door neighbor's Great Dane jumped the fence and chased me down during my six-mile run!"

He continued speaking through the laughter.

"Seriously, though, I did check out a news story about that company a couple of days ago. Good ole Walter C. mentioned it was only a matter of time before those devices that company makes will be able to process information faster than anybody's business. And they say it's going to completely transform how we do almost everything in this country. Now, if that's true, I *am* thinking an investment may not be a bad idea."

"And how much are you thinking?" Admiral Boone asked. "Ten K, twenty?"

At this question, Malcolm's dad bristled, knowing he barely had enough money to make it from one pay check to the next. Investing in theory was a good idea that had not quite approached the doorstep of reality for him.

And, thus, the signal. One clearance of the throat was the customary cue to which Malcolm responded without fail. That night would be no different.

"Daddy, I gotta go," Malcolm said. He tugged his dad's elbow.

"Uh, pardon me, gentlemen," Malcolm's dad said. "I think he's had one cola too many."

"Oh, of course, old boy," Rear Admiral Tate said. "Far be it for us to stand in the way of nature's call."

"We'll be back in two shakes," Malcolm's dad replied.

After they made it home that night, Malcolm's dad would reiterate the importance of always having an exit plan at the ready. Then, he would discuss at length the disdain he harbored for comments made by his white counterparts who dared to compare their experiences with his, especially where they usually endured, at most, a small fraction of the obstacles he'd encountered. The truth was that Rear Admiral Reardon was just one year older than Malcolm's dad when he was elevated to his current rank. By contrast, it would take Malcolm's dad at least five more years before he would seriously be considered Rear Admiral material, despite all the accolades and commendations he'd amassed.

Malcolm's dad had counseled him well on being ever aware that the rules of the game were vastly different for men of their hue and to never let any of the praise, trinkets, and symbols of how "special" they were cloud that fact. His dad then would pivot immediately to statements of how it was still vitally important to advance, grow and learn as much as he could to get to the point where he would become so financially self-sufficient that he would not have to be beholden to others for validation markers. And he taught Malcolm that growth and learning did not stop when the bell rang at the end of the school day or at the end of the workday. Hence, Malcolm's after-hours education sessions among the adults.

* * *

With his olive properly picked and plopped into his cocktail glass, Malcolm wound his way through the throngs of well-dressed lawyers the firm had assembled to welcome the newly inaugurated summer associate class of 1993.His being the only person of color in the class ensured that virtually all those present would know who he was. It also would have placed him at an immediate disadvantage were it not for the hours he'd spent committing to memory the names and faces of all the firm's lawyers in the weeks preceding his first week on the job.

"Malcolm Reid!" the baritone voice bellowed.

Malcolm craned his head to the left and looked over the shoulder of the fellow whose body was next to his. In the distance he spotted the managing partner over whose lips his name spilled so effortlessly.

"Get over here!"

Malcolm smiled. He shifted his cocktail into his left hand and made a beeline to the source of his summons.

"Michael Tannenbaum," Malcolm said. "It is so nice to finally meet you, sir."

Tannenbaum accepted Malcolm's handshake.

"I haven't been knighted by the Queen yet, Reid," Tannenbaum said. "What's with this 'sir' business? Call me Mike like everyone else around here does."

"Sounds good, um, Mike," Malcolm replied.

"So, how are folks treating you here so far, Malcolm?" Tannenbaum asked.

"So far, so good, Mike," Malcolm replied.

"And what have you been working on?" Mike asked. "Sure hope we haven't bored you to death with legal research or some excruciating shit like that."

"Oh, no, sir, I mean, Mike," Malcolm replied. "Forgive me. My dad is in the military, so I'm...."

"No explanation necessary," Tannenbaum said. "I get it. Old habits. As you were saying...."

"No, Mike," Malcolm continued. "All is going well so far. I've got a couple of employment assignments that are keeping me busy, as well as some due diligence for an acquisition."

"Oh, good, good," Tannenbaum said. "Just as long as you're not trapped in research hell. That was all they had us doing back when I was your age and I just hated it. They didn't trust us to do shit. You guys have got it good these days."

"Agreed," Malcolm replied. "We do. But, that's not to say I don't have my share of research, though, Mike. Because I do."

"How in the hell did you get way over here, Mike!?" the high-pitched female voice exclaimed.

"Oh, shit," Tannenbaum whispered. "She found me. And here she comes. Follow my lead when she gets here, Malcolm."

"Um, sure," Malcolm replied.

The five-foot seven-inch blonde-haired beauty sauntered towards Tannenbaum and smiled. Crow's feet gathered at the corner of her eyes as she did so. Tannenbaum spoke.

"Malcolm Reid please meet—" Tannenbaum began.

"Marsha Campbell," Malcolm interrupted. He extended his right hand. "Pleased to meet you, ma'am."

"Likewise," Campbell replied. She looked at Malcolm's hand, declined to shake, then turned to Tannenbaum.

"So, as I was saying earlier before I lost you, Mike," Campbell began. "Arnie has decided he's going to include Regina in his fourth spot for Saturday's scramble, not me. Can you believe it?"

"Has he, now?" Tannenbaum replied. He turned briefly towards Malcolm with a "who cares" expression on his face.

"Yes, he has," Campbell continued. "Now, you know how long I've been vying for that spot, Mike. And, I've been working on my game, so there's absolutely no reason why he—"

"Well, I can talk to him if you want," Tannenbaum interrupted.

"Would you, Mike?" Ms. Campbell asked, smiling. "That would mean the world...."

"Or," Tannenbaum continued. "You could play on *my* foursome. I mean, I'm still putting together my team and have two slots. I was hoping. Wait a second."

"What?" Campbell asked.

"Reid, what's your handicap?"

"My handicap?" Malcolm asked.

"Yep, your golf handicap. Can't be as bad as mine."

Grateful to his dad for so many things that would come in handy during his adult years, chief among them was his instruction in golf. He'd fought the idea of playing the sport for years believing watching paint dry would be a far more interesting way to spend the day. As time went on, however, Malcolm eventually relented and took up the game. Lessons on the Navy base had been free and he found he could play as many rounds as he wanted, especially during times when the base was virtually empty while sailors were deployed for months on end.

"My handicap's pretty bad, Mike," Malcolm replied. "It's about a twenty."

"A twenty!" Tannenbaum said. "You'd kick my ass! But, that's okay. You're playing on my team this Saturday. Is that okay?"

"Sure is," Malcolm said, smiling.

"Okay, how about it, then, Marsha?" Mike asked. "You in too?"

"I'm in!" Campbell exclaimed.

"Okay, good," Tannenbaum said. "Good ole Tommy Haines from tax is going to be our fourth and his game's about as much in the pisser as mine is. But, that's okay, I guess. We'll just have to make sure the beverage cart stays close by so we can drown our sorrows if we have to."

"Indeed," Campbell replied.

"Speaking of," Tannenbaum said, holding up his glass. "I'm empty. I'm going for a refill. Anybody need anything?"

"No, sir, um, I mean, Mike," Malcolm said.

"Marsha?" Tannenbaum asked.

"No, I'm good," Campbell replied.

"Okay, then. I'll catch up with you two a bit later, then," Tannenbaum said. He turned towards Campbell and raised his index finger. "Marsha, be nice."

"So," Campbell began. "From which minority placement program did you come?"

"Excuse me?" Malcolm replied.

"I assume *you* must be here as a result of some type of an affirmative action plan of some sort," Campbell said. "Which one was it?"

"Actually, ma'am," Malcolm began. "I received *my* employment offer through the on-campus interview program. With that said, if the firm does accept students for your fall class through any minority placement programs, that's good to know. I'll be sure to spread the word to some of my friends at school."

"Well, um, I'm not exactly sure we accept students from any such programs or not," Campbell said. "I really was just speculating. Are you the first in your family to attend law school?"

"As a matter of fact, I am," Malcolm replied. "And, I'm pretty excited about finally getting to explore the prospect of developing a career that is not only financially lucrative, but also socially impactful."

"Oh, how very philanthropic of you," Campbell said. "On a different note, has anyone told you where we are dining tonight? I surely hope it won't be here. The wine list at this restaurant is limited and ghastly!"

"You know, I'm not sure," Malcolm replied. "But, if we are dining here, I did some research and it seems this restaurant does have quite an impressive wine cellar in the lower floors of this building. If all else fails, I'm sure the sommelier would be more than willing to recommend options beyond the regular menu that will suit your taste."

As Malcolm concluded his statement, a well-heeled cocktail waitress offered menus to him and Campbell before moving along to the next group of attorneys to do the same.

"Ah, ask and ye shall receive," Campbell said. "Hmm, looks like we *are* eating here after all, but it seems we're deviating from their usual menu tonight. Thank God! Oh, look at the appetizers! What will you be having, Malcolm? The foie gras or the escargot?"

Campbell could have been speaking in Mandarin for all Malcolm knew. It certainly would have made more sense to him than whatever it was she was saying at that moment. He reached into his pocket to partially remove his pager and with one discrete tap, the device came to life. He lifted the pager.

"Westlaw rep," Malcolm said, pointing to the pager. "I've been in the queue with a query I made earlier today for some employment research I'm doing and they're finally getting back to me."

"Oh," Campbell replied.

"I have a tomorrow morning deadline to complete a legal memo, which means I may have to head back to the office after dinner."

The pager continued to buzz.

"My apologies, but do you mind if I go try to find a pay phone to deal with this?" Malcolm asked.

"By all means," Campbell replied. "I certainly understand. Duty calls."

Malcolm excused himself and began to head towards the pay phones near the restrooms with pager in one hand and dinner menu and cocktail glass competing for space in the other. A consultation with the dictionary he kept in his car's glove box would come to the rescue in a matter of minutes, providing him the information he needed to order appetizers and dinner. But, first, after reaching the pay phones, he glanced back towards his former conversation partner, who had already commenced a new conversation with someone else. She whispered into her new conversation partner's ear, who would later whisper into the ears of some of their other colleagues. They craned their necks in Malcolm's general direction, smiled and waved. Malcolm pointed at the pay phone receiver that was glued to his ear and shrugged his shoulders for effect. He waved back.

With each move he'd made that evening, Malcolm would set new standards by which his fellow clerks would be judged. He smiled, hoping his dad would be pleased with his efforts. In keeping with tradition, he'd call his dad hours later to summarize the evening's events. Until then, he continued his faux phone call, eyed the stairwell near the restrooms and considered his next exit strategy that would allow him the crucial minutes he needed to get to his car in the parking garage so he could access the definitions of foie gras and escargot.

***

Confident and engaging conversationalist with a willingness to sacrifice social interaction for work.

These words, among others, would find their way into Marsha Campbell's end-of-summer evaluation of Malcolm Reid, thereby solidifying his offer of post-graduate full-time employment, pending bar exam passage.

***

Twenty-five plus years later, Malcolm Reid would often recount his summer associate experience with his partners during the firm's annual diversity and inclusion symposia in an ongoing effort to shed light on issues of implicit bias and privilege that continued to creep into the firm's hiring decisions well into the new century. He tried to embrace the burden of doing so, realizing that the luxury of relaxing into the twilight of a legal career punctuated by tremendous successes was, unfortunately, one to which he felt he was not entitled. So, his work continued.

He pushed back the chair in which he sat at the conclusion of the firm's 2021 diversity and inclusion forum, stepped off the dais and was immediately approached by a group of young law students with skin tones similar to his own. The firm had increased to three the number of students of color it admitted to its summer associate program that year.

"Mr. Reid," one of the students said. "We wondered if you might have time for lunch or a coffee with us over the next few days. We'd like to hear more about your summer associate experience at the firm and maybe get your thoughts on what we can do to maximize our experience here."

"Well, of course," Malcolm Reid replied, smiling. "I've got about an hour until my next conference call. Why don't we walk across the street, grab some coffee, and chat now? My treat."

The student turned towards his two companions who signaled their agreement in an instant.

"That sounds great," the student said. "We appreciate you taking the time."

"My pleasure," Malcolm Reid replied. "Let's go."

LAUGHS

THE CASE

"What he look like, girl?"

"A damn mess!" Sonia exclaimed. "That's really what he look like!"

Not known for her diplomacy or tact, the bluntness with which the first-year law student described the man who'd courted her for the better part of a month surprised no one. And, as was usually the case, it triggered immediate laughter among the brood of brown beauties that encircled her. Raul Lopez sat silently on the sidelines of her small group that had gathered in the student lounge. He attempted, without success, to stay focused on the case he'd waited until the eleventh hour to read. With ten minutes until the start of the mental and verbal torture that awaited him in the students' tort class, he had no time to waste. After all, his professor had pretty much assured him she'd be calling on him first when the class resumed their discussion of negligence.

"Can you ladies keep it down, please?" Raul asked. "I need to concentrate."

"Boy, you can concentrate yo' ass right outta this lounge if we distractin' you!" Shari exclaimed. "We tryin' to get the scoop on what happened with Don Juan last night. And I *know* you wanna find out just as much as we do. I saw the way you was lookin' when Sonia put him on the speaker phone last week."

"Si, mami, si!" Raul replied. "He sounded muy guapo, pero Professor Solis won't care about how he looked in person when she starts preguntándome about the elements of the negligence claim in this case I'm reading."

"The elements of the claim in the case?" Sonia asked. "I'll tell you about the elements of the claim in the case!"

"Tell him, girl," Shari said.

"Well, first of all," Sonia began. "Based on how this brutha first stepped to me on the phone—"

"And when did that happen?" Denise interrupted.

"Denise, you all late," Shari replied. "We can't be traveling back in time to bring you up to speed. Raul's right! The class starts in less than fifteen minutes."

"Okay, go ahead," Denise said.

"As I was sayin'," Sonia continued, "based on the way he sounded on Reggie's phone when Reggie handed it to me after class *about a month ago.*"

She glared at Denise as she made the statement.

"And y'all *do* remember how Reggie told me one of his boys wanted to meet me after seeing my picture, right?"

"Yes, Sonia, we remember," Shari replied. "Go on, girl."

"Well, anyway, based on what he was sayin' when Reggie handed me his phone and introduced us, I'd say this brutha had a duty to be fine."

"Yep, I agree," Shari replied. "He definitely owed you that."

"Especially with the way he built himself up to be the cutest thing around since Tyson—*after* he got his teeth fixed, that is."

"Not post-dental-work Tyson!" Denise laughed. "Girl, stop!"

"I mean, based on the way he described himself, I would have been crazy not to give him the digits, you know?" Sonia asked.

"Uh-huh," Sonia said. "Y'all know it's been a minute since I broke up with Jakeem and I deserve a little happiness just like anybody else, especially with the stress we dealing with in our first year!"

"Amen," Shari replied.

"Y'all know what I'm talking 'bout."

The crew nodded in affirmation.

"Well, anyway," Sonia continued. She dipped her right hand into the depths of her purse to remove her phone. "Like I said, he had a duty to be what he made himself out to be and I'd say he breached that duty when he ended up lookin' like this."

She held up her phone screen so the group could see.

"Girl, tell me that ain't really him!" Denise exclaimed.

"That's really him," Sonia replied.

"Girl, that's not him!" Shari exclaimed. "That's Flava Dave!"

Guffaws flooded every inch of the airspace in the student lounge. Sonia gathered herself and continued.

"Now, y'all stop with the side comments. I'm tryin' to make the case to the boy! And we ain't got but five minutes left."

"Go on, then," Shari said.

"He breached the duty he owed to me to be fine by turnin' out to be anything but. Y'all agree?"

"Si, Sonia, we agree," Raul replied.

"Okay, so now I got two elements left," Sonia said. "Y'all come up here real close to me and look at my face."

The group leaned in to get a closer look at their friend.

"Now, looka here," Sonia began, pointing to her right eye. "See the way my eye twitchin'?"

"Uh-huh," Shari replied.

"Well, it ain't stopped twitchin' since I came face-to-face with the brutha last night and now I got to go to the doctor to get it checked out!"

"Girl, you crazy!" Denise exclaimed.

"I ain't crazy," Sonia began. "He did this to me! I'm injured! I'm damaged! And, y'all know I don't have insurance. And who knows how much it's gonna cost to fix me?"

"Girl, you are a nut!" Shari screamed.

"Duty, breach, causation and damage," Sonia said. "I got all the elements of my claim. Case closed!"

Having been properly schooled by its leader on the elements of a claim for negligence, the group scooped up its belongings quickly, stuffed backpacks, and exited the student lounge en route to class with less than two minutes to spare.

GIRLS

Who could have predicted Sidney's monosyllabic response to a question would alter the trajectory of her "rising star" status within the cocoon of coolness she'd worked so hard to infiltrate since her transfer to Woodlawn High? Not Sidney. After all, she had no reason to doubt the sincerity of her classmate's interest in wanting firsthand insight into the creative genius behind the makeup designs and wardrobe pairings that had caused cocoon members to swoon with envy. That the girl likely had designs of appropriating some of Sidney's ideas for herself was beside the point. The fact that she'd give Sidney *any* time from her highly coveted social calendar was all that mattered.

"Now that you have my attention, why don't I just pop over to your place after school so you can show me what else you've been—?" Jasmine Hightower began.

The word "sure" launched from Sidney's lips like a cannon before the girl could finish her sentence.

"Eager much?" the girl asked.

"Maybe a little," Sidney replied.

"Well, that's understandable, I guess." The girl peered over the rim of the designer frames that bridged her perfectly shaped nose.

All the research Sidney had done on what made the self-appointed queen of the cocoon tick could not have prepared her for the girl's visit. Sidney knew something was amiss the moment the girl entered the house and stopped next to the window. The twitch of her perfectly shaped nose gave it away.

"What's that smell?" she asked.

"What smell?" Sidney replied.

"You don't smell that?" the girl asked. "Wait a minute. Do old people live here?"

"Well, yeah," Sidney replied. "My grandma lives in our guest room upstairs. She's at her weekly doctor's appointment right now, but—"

The girl showed Sidney the palm of her hand, stopping her midsentence.

"That explains it," she said. "And I take it you guys don't have a housekeeper?"

"Um, no," Sidney replied.

"Hmmm. It shows," the girl said.

She wiped a layer of dust from the windowsill.

"Well, you wanna get started? I'm so excited to show you this color combo I came up with last night!"

"You know, I just remembered," the girl began. "I've got to go pick up my little brother from his chess club. Maybe another time."

"Okay," Sidney replied. "How about tomorrow?"

"My schedule's pretty jammed tomorrow. Let me get back to you."

"Okay," Sidney replied.

The girl breezed past Sidney's front door like the wind, but not before a small, but familiar white slip of paper with numbers and a decimal point caught Sidney's eye. It was fastened to the girl's sweater with only the thinnest piece of plastic.

"Hey, Jasmine!" Sidney said.

"Yes?"

"Don't forget to remove the tag from your sweater!" Sidney glared at the girl. "Unless you plan on returning it, that is!"

"Um, thanks," the girl replied. Redness spread across her perfectly shaped nose.

"Anytime," Sidney said. She closed the door behind her.

THE CHLOE CHRONICLES

"Did I call you?" the three-and-a-half-year old chirped, as she diverted her attention from the vibrant screen images with which she previously had been mesmerized. She immediately locked eyes on the laundry toting five-foot-six-inch creature who invaded her inner sanctum.

Shocked by such a query coming from the mouth of the being who, less than a year earlier, cringed at the thought of being left alone in her own room, Olivia stopped dead in her tracks as if she had encountered a brick wall. Openmouthed, Olivia turned toward her daughter and maneuvered her right hand away from the warmth of the freshly dried garments she carried until it found her hip.

"Look, I can come into your room whenever I want to come into your room," Olivia said. "Besides, I need to put these clothes away. Don't make me come over there and take that tablet away."

Olivia could not recall the exact moment in her almost four-year history with Chloe when their relationship had morphed from one in which Olivia was encouraging her apprehensive daughter to exert her independence to that in which she felt the need to justify her actions in response to her offspring's obvious attempt to stake a claim to her newfound territory. Whenever it was, Olivia was not sure if she was quite ready to deal with this new aspect of her daughter's personality.

If she's like this at three and a half, what in the world will she be like at sixteen, Olivia thought.

Chloe released the tablet, steered her left hand upward to point to Olivia and giggled in response to Olivia's statement.

"Mommy, you're funny!" She lifted her bare feet and wriggled her toes for emphasis.

Olivia was taken aback again, this time by the swiftness with which her daughter transformed back into the toddler she had to coax to bed hours earlier. In an instant, Olivia felt a bit embarrassed for threatening to remove the device that, over the past several months, had served as the perfect bargaining chip to get her daughter to settle down for bed.

Watch one show, then lights out.

This was the offer Olivia had made during those first few nights she attempted to persuade her daughter to begin sleeping in her own room. Fortunately for Olivia, Chloe agreed.

Olivia was equally thankful that, in this current moment, Chloe interpreted Olivia's statement about removing the device as a joke. Now, if only Olivia could convince herself of the same.

Sure, it was a joke, Olivia thought.

What had not been a joke, however, was how challenging the past three years had been for Olivia, as she assumed the responsibility of rearing her daughter as a single mother. It was a rare occurrence for Olivia to revisit the conversation a year and a half earlier that altered the trajectory of her life and that of her daughter forever—the conversation she had with her ex-husband when he rather matter-of-factly told Olivia he simply did not want to be married anymore.

From that moment forward, Olivia knew she would have to brace herself for the challenging times that lay ahead. And she did. She pressed the pause button on any thought of having much of a social life of her own to steer the lion's share of her efforts, outside of her demanding career, toward making sure Chloe had as much of a *normal* life as possible under the circumstances. To Olivia's credit, Chloe had begun to mature into the well-adjusted, smart, loving giggle box that sat before her on this night.

Olivia closed the door to the armoire that housed the last of tonight's wash. She climbed into bed to join her daughter, who minutes earlier somehow managed to usher away the giggle fairies that had invaded her body so she could return to the show she had been watching on her tablet.

"What are you watching, Love?" Olivia asked.

"Dora, Mommy," Chloe replied. "I'm watching Dora."

"Okay," Olivia said. "Can I watch too?"

"Yes, abs, abso, absolutely," Chloe replied.

"Great word, Chloe," Olivia said. She elevated her hand to invite a high five, which invitation was swiftly accepted by the palm of the small figure tucked snuggly next to her.

Olivia and Chloe continued watching the last fifteen minutes of Dora's latest *aventura*. Olivia gently stroked the thick strands of hair that had been a bit of an adventure for Olivia and her brush earlier that day. She considered how blessed she was to have such a resilient child. To be sure, the past couple of years could not have been a cake walk for her little girl, with Olivia having to shuttle her between her home and her ex-husband's apartment on alternating weekends. Not to mention having to alternate families every year during the major holidays. That was one thing that tore Olivia up the most about finally deciding to end her marriage. She had said as much to her own mother when she sought her counsel before making the decision to divorce.

She will have to split time between our family and his, Olivia had said. *And I don't want that for her.*

In the end, Olivia knew any attempt to maintain a sham of a marriage for her daughter's sake would have been far worse and undoubtedly would have led to certain doom for them both, especially if the deterioration she experienced during those final days of the relationship were any indication.

Children, especially those at her age, pick up on things, Olivia's mother had said. She was right.

And so, for her sake and for Chloe's, Olivia decided to end it. Chloe was almost two. Following the initial adjustment to not having her daddy around on a daily basis, Chloe began to handle the breakup like a trooper.

During the first days after the breakup as she sensed Olivia's exasperation at having to shoulder alone the tasks she previously shared with her ex-husband, Chloe took it upon herself to be especially helpful to Olivia. Olivia noted the manner in which Chloe made an extra effort to organize her toys by herself after playtime upon being prompted only once by Olivia's "clean up" song. It previously had been her ex-husband's job to assist with the task. She also appreciated the way Chloe sat patiently to watch one of her shows or played quietly when it was Olivia's turn to go into the bathroom in the mornings for a shower. It previously had been her ex-husband's job to keep Chloe occupied during Olivia's bathroom time.

Can you sit here for a few minutes while Mommy takes a shower? Olivia would ask.

Yes, Mommy, Chloe would reply.

And that would be that.

Despite these signs of self-sufficiency and maturity, Olivia recalled her own initial apprehension at the thought of creating some semblance of a personal life for herself outside of life with her daughter. As she transitioned her hand from the locks on Chloe's head to the upper part of her back, Olivia remembered how she had balked at the mere suggestion of becoming involved with another man when one of her best friends began to coax Olivia to dip her toe into the dating pool about a year ago.

Absolutely not, Olivia had said. *How would Chloe react?*

Girl, that little lady is far more mature than you might think, Olivia's friend had replied.

After several phone conversations with that same friend in addition to more than a few talks with her mother, Olivia decided to throw caution to the wind. She agreed to her friend's invitation to meet someone new. The chemistry between Olivia and the new man in her life was immediate. Chloe's comfort level with him was almost just as immediate. Instead of exhibiting signs of resistance or jealousy, Chloe encouraged the relationship. Sensing Olivia's desire for some alone time with her new male friend, Chloe would manage to excuse herself often with statements of *Mommy, I'm sleepy* or *Mommy, can I go play?* Throughout Olivia's courtship, Chloe even helped to break through the obvious tension that hung in the air between Olivia and her ex-husband when the latter got wind of Olivia's dating, and eventual engagement, to the new man.

The comment Chloe made upon her daddy's meeting Olivia's new fiancé for the first time at Olivia's house was priceless.

You see, Daddy, I told you that you were going to like him, she had said.

Laughter echoed throughout the house at the statement. It was official. The ice had been broken. That is not to say, however, that everything had gone smoothly. There were more than a few bumps in the road. The incident that occurred on Olivia's wedding day was a prime example.

Olivia's wedding day to her new fiancé, by all appearances, could not have been any more picture perfect. The weather was mild and sunny, the wedding party arrived on time, the flowers were beautiful. The only "wild card," which Olivia freely admitted, would be Chloe. Would she or wouldn't she fulfill the role specially created for her—flower girl? She would not. Olivia, sensing whether Chloe would or would not cooperate could have easily been decided by the flip of a coin, took Chloe's decision in stride. She did not become flustered by that decision at all or by the other incident that occurred—one that caught several of Olivia's wedding guests off guard.

Are you sure? Olivia had asked Chloe minutes before the start of the ceremony.

Yes, Mommy, I'm sure, Chloe had replied.

Well, okay, Olivia had said.

So, the ceremony began. While Chloe already had abdicated her role as flower girl minutes before Olivia's latest query, based on the excitement Chloe had displayed during wedding rehearsal, Olivia was much more optimistic about the likelihood that Chloe would participate in the sand pouring component of the ceremony. The ritual required Olivia, her fiancé, and Chloe to pour sand from three small glasses into one larger vase as a symbol of the three of their lives being joined into one.

To Olivia's chagrin, five minutes before that portion of the wedding ceremony began, Chloe interrupted the solemnity of the proceedings with one exclamation.

I have to go potty!

More than a handful of wedding guests all heard the statement, as evidenced by the audible gasps that escaped the lips of some of them. Olivia would later thank her older brother for springing to action and whisking Chloe out of the sanctuary to address her immediate issue only to bring her daughter back just in time to participate in the sand pouring ceremony.

Think nothing of it, her brother, through laughter, had said in reply.

And so, Olivia's new life with her new husband and Chloe began.

With about five minutes left in Dora's *aventura*, Olivia could not help but contemplate what other adventures lay ahead for her and her new family. Chloe's comment upon Olivia's entering the room on this night certainly signaled there would be many, many more. Olivia smiled and began to ponder the specifics of what they might be, when she was interrupted yet again by the same chirping sound that had greeted her earlier.

"You can go now, Mommy," Chloe said. She removed Olivia's hand from the middle of her spine.

"Okay," Olivia replied. She began to unfold her limbs in preparation to rise from Chloe's bed. When she reached Chloe's bedroom door, Olivia glanced at her daughter one last time before she left, noting the familiar giggle that escaped Chloe's lips. A smile crept across Olivia's face as she exited her daughter's room en route to spend some alone time with her new husband.

Chloe redirected her attention to her tablet screen, relishing the thought of enjoying a few last minutes of her own alone time before turning in for bed.

TRYIN'

"That ain't even funny," Lamiracle sneered.

Jaquinten sucked his teeth before snatching from his sister the screenplay on which he'd worked for the better part of six months. Not naturally inclined to think quickly on his feet, a full thirty seconds elapsed before he could muster the mental fortitude to clap back.

"That shit *is* funny!" he replied. "Just because yo' ass don't got no sense of humor don't mean dis not gon' be a hit!"

Bypassing her brother's insult for the moment, Lamiracle instead aimed to attack an area where she knew he was vulnerable.

"'Don't got no!'" she exclaimed. "First of all, learn how to speak proper English! Did you mean to say 'don't have any sense of humor?'"

"Don't start with me, La La," Jaquinten replied. "Dis just me and you sittin' up in here. I left my teacher at school three hours ago. Anyway, you sho' not cornering the market on good grammar either. Didn't you just say 'That ain't even funny?'"

"Whatevah, nigga," Lamiracle snapped. "Let's get back to the issue at hand. All I'm sayin' is you asked me to read this and give you my honest opinion and I'm givin' it to you."

"Okay, okay," Jaquinten said. "That's fair. I did ask you for that. But, you ain't told me why you don't think it's funny."

"That's because you didn't give a sistah a chance, man," Lamiracle replied. "As usual, you got all defensive and sensitive instead. If you want me to tell you what's wrong with it, I will."

"Okay, okay, tell me," Jaquinten said.

"Well, for starters, this story just seems too ordinary for me."

"What you mean by that?" Jaquinten asked.

"Well, look like all you did was describe what happened last summer when cousin Pee-Wee told us how he got chased down by that dog he was tryin' to catch when he was working dat dog catchin' job. You know, the story about how the dog turned on him and made him run all the way down the street 'til he was rescued at Aunt Bertha's house 'cause she opened the door for him just in time?"

"Yeah, yeah, so you picked up on that, right?" Jaquinten asked, smiling.

"Um, yeah, I picked up on that," Lamiracle replied. "Yo' description about what happened was almost exactly the same as Pee-Wee's. All you did was change the names."

"Exactly," Jaquinten said.

"So, um, what's so funny 'bout that?" Lamiracle asked. "At the time Pee-

Wee told us dat story, we was just happy he didn't git bit by dat dog. He lost his job and was outta work for three months because of that."

"Well, I can see why he lost it," Jaquinten replied. "He was a dog catcher. How you gon' be a dog catcher and afraid of dogs?"

"Whatevah, Quint," Lamiracle replied. "By the way, that dog could've had rabies or who knows what!"

"But it didn't catch him, La La, so we'll never know! He was fine!" Jaquinten exclaimed. "Let's get back to my story. The fact that I changed the dog from a German shepherd to a poodle—you didn't think that was funny either?"

"Uh, uh, no," Lamiracle replied.

"Well, dat's why I say you don't got no sense of humor," Jaquinten said. "'Cause dat shit funny. Just picture it!"

"No. It. Ain't!" Lamiracle exclaimed. "All you doin' is describing real life stuff anyway. Anybody can do dat."

"Maybe they can," Jaquinten said. "But, they not. Except for dat one brutha who made dat show on cable that's been winnin' all them awards. What's his name?"

"What show?" Lamiracle asked.

"You know that one 'bout dat brutha who tried to convince his rapper cousin to let him be his manager. He dropped his cousin's mix tape at the radio station. You know what I'm talkin' 'bout."

"Aw, yeah," Lamiracle replied. "You talkin' 'bout that show with that different actin' brutha' who was used to be a rapper in real life?"

"Yep," Jaquinten said. "Him. Look at him. All it look like he did was take some real-life shit and find some regular looking people—not them Hollywood beautiful people—and he just wrote about his own shit."

"Yeah," Lamiracle replied. "Dat's *all* he did. And dat shit ain't funny either."

"Then, why dat show been winnin' so many awards?" Jaquinten asked. "If it ain't funny, as you say?"

"I don't know," Lamiracle replied. "Who be decidin' on what shows get to win the awards anyway?"

"Hollywood!" Jaquinten exclaimed. "Them folks in Hollywood."

"Do any of them folks look like us, or think like us?" Lamiracle asked.

"I don't know," Jaquinten replied. "I don't think so."

"Then, there you go!" Lamiracle exclaimed.

"There you go—what?" Jaquinten asked.

"That explain everything," Lamiracle replied. "Them folks in Hollywood don't know what's funny."

"Yes, they do," Jaquinten argued. "You don't know that you talkin' 'bout."

"No, they don't," Lamiracle replied. "They don't experience life the way I do, so what's funny to them most times ain't gon' be funny to me," Lamiracle said. "And you know, most of them just tryin' to take our shit and make some money off it. They been doin' it for years. They tryin' to capitalize on our experience so they can keep gettin' paid while we keep sittin' here in the ghetto. Instead of makin' all that money laughin' at our hardship, why ain't they figuring out a way to steer all that money in our community so we can get a piece of the pie for a change?"

"Now, here you go gittin' all deep and philosophical and shit," Jaquinten said. "All I'm tryin' to do is write somethin' to give folks a chance to take a break and laugh for a few minutes out of the day. Besides, it's a brutha dat's makin' bank and getting' the awards for writin' about his own shit, not dem white folks in Hollywood."

"Uh, hmm," Lamiracle replied. "And, if dat brutha makin' ten million off dat show, I'm sure dem white folks makin' twenty times dat."

"Damn, La La," Jaquinten began. "Why you always gotta go and find a way to bring me down when I'm tryin' to figure out a way to pull all us up outta here?"

"I'm all for tryin' to figure out a way to pull us up," Lamiracle said. "I'm just not sure giving white folks another reason to point and laugh at us like we some animals in a zoo is the way to do it."

"Well, I don't care what you say," Jaquinten replied. "I'm gon' keep writin' and tryin' to figure out a way to get these coins, 'cause—"

"La La, Quint!" the high-pitched, scratchy-voiced elderly lady exclaimed. "Y'all get on up here to this kitchen so you can help me cut this government cheese! It's hard as a brick again and you know I cain't cut it myself on account of my arthritis! You remember I darn near fell ovah the last time I tried! Get on up here now while I go put my teeth in! I'm hungry! Y'all ain't had nothin' since you got outta school. I know you must be hungry too!"

Lamiracle and Jaquinten turned their eyes away from the staircase that would transport them from the basement in which they sat to the kitchen, then towards each other before laughter flooded the room.

"Write that down!" Lamiracle exclaimed.

"You know I am!" Jaquinten replied.

PERSPECTIVE

THE CYCLE

In the twenty years since this reunited group's cheers and roars routinely ushered its varsity basketball team from one victory to the next, on this night, screams of recognition, delight and surprise cascade from the rafters of the Hanover High School gymnasium like New Year's Eve confetti in Times Square.

"Girl, you look so good!" Carmen squeals. Her arms encircle the shoulders of her former high school tormentor. She scrolls her eyes from head to toe of Leah Maxwell's five-foot-three inch, two-hundred-pound frame, smiles and lies. "You have not changed one bit."

Carmen recalls Leah's taut, six-pack-abbed seventeen-year-old body and, for a moment, wonders if the image she holds of her "frenemy" is misplaced. She looks past Leah's left shoulder and focuses on the large screen mounted to the wall behind the basketball goal to see a petite Leah and her familiar smile, standing atop one of many cheerleading pyramids she'd scaled as a teen. Leah observes Carmen's attention stray from her and focus on the screen. Leah inclines her index finger towards the screen, laughs, lifts her jacket and redirects her finger to the additional layer of flesh that surrounds the entirety of her midriff.

"Before and after, girl," Leah laughs. "Before. And. After."

"Girl, stop!" Carmen exclaims. She fake smiles. "You know you still look good."

"In the face maybe," Leah replies. "Other than that... not so much. But enough about me."

Leah eagerly reaches down into her designer handbag and removes her smartphone. She taps the screen to illuminate the images displayed within. She tilts the screen towards Carmen.

"Are these your...?" Carmen begins.

"My munchkins?" Leah replies. "Yes, girl. That's Regina. She's thirteen. And that's Damian. He's eight."

"Oh wow! They are precious, Leah," Carmen says.

"That they are," Leah replies. "But, as you can see, they fucked my body up!"

Carmen pushes aside the specious claim that having her last child eight years ago could result in the borderline obese state of the person fronting her.

"Girl, if you don't stop, you gon' have me lying on this floor!" Carmen exclaims.

"But, it's true," Leah lies. "This old bag of bones snapped back after baby number one. But, after Damian? Not so much."

"So, you gained a little weight," Carmen says. "Who cares? At least you have your babies to show for it. I couldn't have any."

"Girl, that's too bad," Leah says. "Have you seen Alex Watson yet? Rumor has it his wife left him for another man."

"No, I haven't seen him," Carmen replies. "As I was saying, I couldn't have children because the doctor told me that...."

"Did you say something, girl?" Leah asked. "It's hard to hear with that music blasting and all these people trying to get my attention."

Leah notices her cheerleading clique has cocooned itself in the auditorium's far side corner.

"I was telling you why I can't have children!" Carmen yells.

"Oh, girl, I'm sorry about that," Leah says.

"Don't apologize," Carmen replies. "It's not your fault."

"It's just that here I am going on and on about me and—"

"Let me stop you there," Carmen begins. "You don't have to show fake concern or pity for me. I'm very happy with where I am in my life. Besides, I'd expect nothing less than for you to focus on yourself and how in demand you still are for attention. After all, you've got a reputation to uphold, right? I'm just glad you found time to talk to me."

Leah slowly elevates her bottom lip so that it meets her upper one, as she realizes Carmen's words had caused her mouth to fall open.

"What do you mean by that?" Leah asks.

"I mean, you were the captain of the cheerleading team, you were Homecoming Queen. I get it. There must be a lot of pressure coming back after all this time and knowing that most, if not all, of your classmates will be monitoring your every move, not to mention every curve of your physique for the slightest imperfection. Too bad you're giving them something to laugh about this year instead of something to admire."

"What?!" Leah exclaims. She allows her eyes to leave Carmen's, then scans the room to witness her classmates' raised eyebrows and covert glares, many of whom unsuccessfully cup their mouths to conceal the whispers and giggles from also coming into view.

"And I must confess I am somewhat surprised that I don't feel as satisfied as I thought I would at this moment," Carmen says.

"What moment?" Leah asks.

"The moment I get to tell you how absolutely thrilled I am with how my life turned out, despite your best efforts to make me and others like me feel like shit when we were growing up."

"I didn't—" Leah begins.

"Oh, yes you did," Carmen interjects. "Like the time I came to school with my first pair of glasses, the frames for which I admit were a bit dated. It was all my parents could afford at the time. What was it you said? Oh yeah—'Guys don't make passes at girls that wear glasses.' And, then you added something about my weight. What was it? Oh, yeah. 'Or girls with wide asses.'"

Carmen opens her jacket and runs the palms of her hands over the contours of her firm, tight butt, while staring at the flabby backside Leah unsuccessfully attempts to conceal by pulling down her designer sweater.

"I believe you were with your cheerleading crew when you hurled that particular insult at me," Carmen continues. "Is that them over in the corner? Yes, it is. I remember like it was yesterday how hard they laughed at that one."

Images of a smiling Leah leading the Homecoming Court down the football field during senior year, her tiara perched atop her head, flash across the big screen.

"Or, how about the time you dared Sebastian O'Brien to kiss me behind the band director's office door?" Carmen asks. "I'll never forget that picture of me with the 'I MADE OUT WITH STUPID' sign Sebastian taped to my back when he wrapped his arm around me for our 'lip lock.' I didn't even feel it when he stuck that sign on my back. His kiss made my day all those years ago, that is until I saw that picture of my back with that sign stuck to it. If memory serves, it was projected up on the same screen we're looking at now. During one of our pep rallies, right? I still can't figure out how you managed to pull that one off."

"I am so sorry about that, girl." Carmen says. "It was just...."

"Again, Leah, no need to be sorry," Carmen replies. "I look back on those episodes and I can laugh about them now, just as some of our classmates appear to be pointing and laughing at you now. Oh, look, I think that's Sebastien O'Brien!"

Leah scans the room until she finds the bleachers. Sebastien O'Brien and his football buddies glare at her, their middle-aged and bloated bodies doubled over in laughter. Tears begin to roll down Leah's cheeks.

"But, as I said before," Carmen begins without a hint of sincerity. "You still look good, girl. Your face is just as beautiful as ever. Not a blemish in sight."

Leah bolts out of the gymnasium en route to the ladies' room. Carmen begins to circulate the room to mingle with her other classmates. The three cocktails she consumes in the fifteen minutes that follow prompt her own exodus to the lavatory. Upon opening the ladies' room door, she hears muffled sounds of two voices spilling over the only occupied stall in the room. One voice is Leah's. The other is someone not in the room. It sounds like Leah's but is scratchier, perhaps older. Carmen inclines her ear towards the stall and hears the voice from the phone speak first.

"And did that trollop Cynthia Berry comes to the reunion this time?"

"Yes, Mama, she's here," Leah replies.

"What she look like?" Leah's mother asks. "She still got that big forehead? A pause.

"Yes," Leah replies, reluctantly.

"And what about that nerdy girl, what was her name? Carey or Carly or something like that?"

"Carmen," Leah replies.

"Yeah," Leah's mother says. "That's it. What about her? She there too?"

"Yes, Mama, she's here," Leah replies.

"She still got them thick Coke bottle glasses she used to wear? You know the ones with them real crazy looking frames?" Leah's mother asks, through laughter. "Man, them glasses were thick! And ugly!"

"No, Mama," Leah replies. "She doesn't have glasses anymore."

Leah begins to cry.

"You cryin'?" Leah's mother asks. "What you cryin' for? Uh-huh. Now you better get yourself together. I didn't raise no weakling. I raised a tough and strong beauty queen! Did you tell me earlier you was calling me from the bathroom? You go to the sink, get in front of that mirror and clean yourself up. Fix your wig and your makeup and get your ass back out there! You need to show them folks you the one still running things around there! Don't let me have to jump in my car and drive down there to snatch you up! You hear?!"

"Bye, Mama," Leah replies.

"Don't you hang up on me 'cause I'm not finished telling you—" Leah's mother begins an instant before Leah silences her by abruptly ending the call.

Leah reaches down into her purse to deposit her smart phone and extract a pill dispenser. She clears her throat before opening the stall door. Carmen quickly hides herself in the stall next to Leah's to conceal the fact that she is eavesdropping. Moments later Carmen slowly opens her stall door. She witnesses Leah ingesting the pill, then bending over to drink from the sink's faucet. Carmen then moves toward the bathroom sink, reaches down into her purse to remove a small bottle of water. She offers the bottle to Leah. Leah shakes her head.

"No, girl. I'm good. But thanks."

Carmen notices and recognizes the pink hue of the candy sized pill before Leah snaps her pill case shut.

"Lexotonin?" Carmen asks.

"Yep," Leah replies. "Forgot to take it earlier, so I thought I would do it now. I'm supposed to take it daily and we still have a couple of hours left before midnight."

A pause.

"Hold on. You know about lexotonin?"

"Sure do," Carmen says. "I took my last dosage about six months ago. And I'm still trying to shake the side effects."

"What side effects did you have?" Leah asks.

"A bit of depression," Carmen replies. She lifts from her handbag a small white bottle and presents it to Leah. "One more week's worth of meds for the side effects. Then, I should be done. And you? Any side effects from the lexotonin?"

"You're looking at it," Leah replies. She opens her arms wide to present an unobstructed view of the entirety of her girth. "It's like there are two of me now."

"Don't worry about that, girl," Carmen says. "You'll lose the weight in time, after you finish with those meds."

"I don't know, girl," Leah replies. "I'm not getting any younger and we all know the older you get the harder it is to lose it. But we'll see. And in the meantime—"

"In the meantime," Carmen interrupts. "You and I should go do something fun tomorrow. A movie maybe? That is, if you are available, girl."

"That sounds like fun," Leah replies. "Can we go see that new one? You know the one that's based on James Baldwin's book?"

"Yep," Carmen says. "I haven't seen that one yet either."

"Wait, wait," Leah says. "Oh, shoot! I forgot I told my mama I would take her to the Alpha Sigma Delta fashion show at the convention center downtown. And my daughter is supposed to go with us. It'll be her first show."

"A fashion show, huh?" Carmen asks. "You still going to those things?"

"Yes, girl," Leah replies. "Mama likes to play the 'spot the fat' game. I'm sure she will bring her laser pointers for all of us."

"Laser pointers?" Carmen asks.

"Yes, girl," Leah replies. "She likes to play this game where we aim the laser pointers at the cellulite on the models. After shining a light on the fat, you have to take a picture with your phone so you have proof of what you saw. Whoever has the most pictures at the end of the show wins."

"Wins what?" Carmen asks.

"Well, the last time we played, the loser had to buy the winner a gift of the loser's choosing, but something the loser thinks the winner needs and can actually use. The last time we played, I won and Mama lost so she had to buy me something."

"So, what did she buy you?" Carmen asks.

"A scale," Leah replies.

Leah tilts her head back and opens her mouth wide to clear a path for the laughter that erupts. Carmen resists the urge but cannot. Ten seconds later, her laughter subsides and she stares at Leah in silence.

"It's really not funny," Leah says.

"No, it's not," Carmen replies. "And the weight gain from the meds you have been taking—does she know that you have...."

"Cancer?" Leah asks. "Yes, but my mama don't care."

"If you don't mind me saying so," Carmen begins, "I always thought she was kind of a—"

"Bitch!" Leah interrupts. "It's okay. You can say it. Everybody knows how she is. And, she's so set in her ways now, she ain't never gon' change."

"Well, alright, then," Carmen says. "Maybe another time for that movie? I'm getting tired, girl, so I think I'm gon' head out. And, about what I said earlier, girl—"

"It's all right, Carmen," Leah says. "I know how I was back then. I deserve it."

"But, two wrongs don't make a right," Carmen replies. "I should know better."

"It's all good, girl," Leah replies. "You don't grow up in a household like mine without developing a thick skin."

"Thick skin or not," Carmen says. "What I said earlier was wrong and I apologize. "

"Apology accepted," Leah replies.

They embrace.

"Bye, girl," Carmen says. She moves toward the door to exit the ladies' room.

"Carmen, wait!" Leah says. "If your offer of a movie still stands, let's go. And do you mind if I bring my daughter?"

"Not at all," Carmen replies.

"Good," Leah says. "I'll call her now to tell her about the change in plans."

She scrolls through her list of contacts to find her daughter's name. She depresses the *face-to-face* feature on her smartphone.

"But, what about your mother?" Carmen asks.

"She grown. Just like I'm grown. I'm sure she will make other arrangements to get to that fashion show if she really wants to go."

"But, won't she be upset?" Carmen asks.

"Probably," Leah replies. "But she'll get over it. She's got thick skin too."

"Okay, then," Carmen says, laughing. "So, I'll text some movie times to you in the morning."

"Sounds good," Leah replies.

The image of her daughter's face appears in Leah's phone screen.

"I'll see you tomorrow, girl," Carmen says. She opens the ladies' room door to exit.

"Yes, you will," Leah replies.

"And, I look forward to meeting your daughter," Carmen says.

Leah's phone screen comes to life to reveal a clear image of her daughter. Leah observes her daughter laughing and pointing a laser towards what appears to be a mannequin in a department store. She hears her mother's familiar laugh and voice in the background coaxing her daughter to practice.

"Don't forget to text me those movie times," Leah replies. "We can be available at your convenience, girl."

SANGUINITY WITH A SIDE OF SILVER FISH

The CEO's electronic edict invaded my inbox with "high importance" as I concluded my third call of the day with the latest executive for whom I'd been tasked with helping close a deal.

"Man, the lawyers on that conference call earlier were shouting so much BS, I wanted to reach through the phone and just strangle 'em!" the executive said. "How you manage to stay so calm and positive during these calls I'll never know."

"Well, that's what you pay me for," I said. "The way I see it is if I respond to their shouts and craziness with my own, I'm playing right into their hands and they win. And…."

"We're not playing to lose!"

"No way, no how!" I replied. "So, now they know where we stand. With another round or two of calls, this deal will be done! Don't worry. All is not lost. Not by a long shot!"

"Good deal. So, what else we got?"

"Well," I began. "The big boss's email just popped up on my screen and—"

"Yeah? You still there?"

"Um, sorry about that," I replied. "Just reading through this. Looks like we're being told to get the heck out of dodge, so the next time I talk to you probably will be from my cell."

"Is that right?"

"Appears so," I replied. "And I think we have less than two hours to leave."

"Well, that's all she wrote! Why don't you give me a call later?"

"Sure thing," I replied.

The loud but muffled female's voice met my ears the moment my phone's receiver met its base.

"Everyone has got a plan 'til they get punched in the mouth!"

"Mike Tyson!" I bellowed, hitting the drywall separating my office from hers.

"Ding, ding, ding!" Marcy Collier screamed. "You got it, brother!"

The twenty-year litigator with a penchant for shouting celebrity quotes at random punctuated her remark with an equally firm swat at her wall.

"Looks like we're outta here!" she exclaimed.

"Yep!"

Initial reports of the pandemic's deadly impact sent shock waves through the office. As I placed the lid on my fourth and final box of legal goodies that would accompany me on my journey across town, silver fish slipped from the inner fold of the box top and fell to the ground. They slithered swiftly toward the dark, moist corner beneath my windowsill.

"Looks like we're not the only ones being kicked out!" Marcy exclaimed.

I jumped.

"Good gravy, lady! You can't just sneak up on a fella like that!" "After all these years working together, you still ain't ready for my stealth moves!"

She kept her distance, peering through the recently installed glass wall fronting my office in observance of recently implemented social distancing rules.

"I guess not!" I replied.

I shook the lid a few more times to ensure no holdover tenants remained, then secured the lid to the box.

"Well, I guess I'll see you when I see you, my friend," she said.

"I'm buying first round at next week's virtual happy hour," I said.

"You mean, if we're not all in the hospital by then," she replied. "Or worse."

"Geesh, you're killing my buzz. Get outta here with that already!"

"Bye, Mulder," she said.

"Bye, Scully," I replied.

* * *

The minute I exited the building's parking garage, furry legs and a tail blazed past my front bumper. My right foot immediately released the accelerator and attacked the brake as if I were smashing glass to signal the end of a Jewish wedding, averting the creature's near-certain death.

"What the flock!" I screamed.

Four deep breaths later I recommenced my trek. Upon arriving home, I steered my car into my driveway. I removed the garage door opener from my visor and pressed the button on the device. Nothing. I pressed again. Nothing.

"Sheet!" I exclaimed.

I parked, popped the trunk, removed two of my four boxes. I walked towards the front door when my keys slid off the top box and hit the ground. I lowered the boxes, scooped up my keys and unlocked the front door. I placed the keys in my left pocket, picked up the boxes and crossed the door's threshold. My right foot's unplanned rendezvous with the leg of my coffee table sent pain from my lower extremity directly to my brain, prompting yet another non-expletive to escape my lips.

"Crap!" I exclaimed. "It's because you never come into the house through the front, stupid! Now, get a grip, suck it up and move on!"

I did. I reached the landing at the top of my staircase. I entered my makeshift office and noticed three rows of boxes stacked five deep beneath the far window. My lips curled upward, as I considered the time self-quarantine would afford me to finish unpacking. I lowered my two office boxes onto one of the stacks of five. I removed the lid from the top box. Three silver fish fell from the lid and slid under the bottom box towards the wall beneath the windowsill.

"No way!" I exclaimed. "You guys are *not* camping out here tonight!"

I started lifting boxes. The last box's bottom gave way the minute it left the ground, causing several books to spill. My high school yearbook topped the pile. I opened the book and was immediately drawn to the wording spread across its inside cover. The disjointed ramblings of my then-best friend's familiar, grammatically challenged script consumed the entirety of the space. I paused when I reached the last paragraph.

No matter where you end up, you can always send me a smoke signal, Kemosabe. And if all else fails, call my old lady (Mom) at the house 'cause we both no she ain't goin' nowhere.

I lifted my smartphone from my pocket. I ignored three 'urgent' texts from the office, accessed the phone's keypad and input the ten digits. I dialed.

MORE THAN ENOUGH

Caleb Campbell stared out the window of his seventh-floor one-bedroom condo watching the furry creatures engage in their morning ritual. The late November South Florida sun parted the cumulus clouds that curtained it, causing the group's leader to gaze up. But, only for a moment, as empty bellies compelled her to spring into action quickly. And she did so on that day, as she did every single day without fail. Caleb marveled at the unrelenting fervor with which the creatures looked out for each other.

He considered the way so many self-actualized adults of his own species had such difficulty doing the same. He knew most of them outwardly proclaimed the near universally accepted belief that the true measure of a life well lived could only ultimately be defined by the quality of one's connections to others, a notion undergirded by the belief that, at the end of the day, humans truly do need other humans to be fulfilled. He also knew that just beneath the desire for human connection resided a gnawing, deep and unyielding sense of lack and a constant longing to be attached to someone outside of ourselves to feel complete.

Or was it some "thing?" Caleb wondered at what point in time the confusion began. When exactly did we begin to substitute the need for some "one" else with the need for some "thing" else? Caleb was certain that the capitalistic society into which he was birthed, with its incessant commercial interference, did not help.

He stepped away from the window, took a seat on his sofa and began to piece together his thoughts by putting pen to paper that Friday morning, one day after he awoke from his self-induced coma, a vestige of the previous day's food fest also known as Thanksgiving. On that day, his family, like most, took time to pause and reflect, between servings, on the many reasons to be grateful. The reflections inevitably coalesced around and rested upon those closest to him who were all assembled at the dinner table—his widowed mother Claudia, his younger brother Christian and his older sister Crystal, together with her husband and two kids. But, then, just a few short hours later, discussions among those with whom he'd gathered and without whom he openly proclaimed his life would not be complete, invariably shifted to how many deals they could find on Black Friday (which actually began on Thursday) and how much discounted "stuff" they'd all be able to squeeze into their online shopping carts.

Television commercials connecting one segment of the day's athletic competitions to the next only reinforced the notion that if they could only get their hands on the next big thing, (on sale for a limited time only), perhaps they'd get that much closer to making their lives complete. But, wait. Was it he and the others with whom he'd gathered that made each other's lives complete? Or the stuff? Fifteen minutes at dinner spent discussing the value of relationships. The next several hours on the value of retail. It was almost as if a Ray Ban bespectacled Will Smith had whipped out his memory stick and erased all thoughts of their earlier protestations in a twisted scene from *Men In Black*.

* * *

The test Caleb devised was rather simple. Its results? Much too hard to predict. He penned a note to each family member with whom he shared in the previous day's Thanksgiving festivities and signed them. The notes requested each family member's presence at his condominium at the appointed time on Christmas Eve. Only by coming to his place would they be able to receive what he hoped they'd view as a special gift. He asked his mother to get there early—for prime seating and, being the only other person on the planet with a key to his place, so she could let the others in. He would absent himself on that day so as not to influence the outcome.

Claudia Campbell arrived at her son's flat at 7:30 a.m. sharp on Christmas Eve. She lifted the key he'd made for her years ago in case of emergencies from her purse, unlocked the door and walked in. On the counter to her immediate right was a handwritten note.

> *Mom, I wanted you to arrive first so you could captain the ship as I observe from the shoreline (also known as the courtyard downstairs). When the rest of the family arrives, please have them each take a pair of the binoculars (somehow, I've managed to accumulate several of them over the years). Please tell them to look out the window facing East at precisely 8:00 a.m. and to focus on the large banyan tree on the opposite side of the hill. One side of the tree will be facing my condo building; the other will be facing the street. They (and you) should aim the binoculars at the bottom of the tree and wait. The entire thing should last about 15 minutes. Thank you so much for doing this and Merry Christmas! Your son, Caleb.*

* * *

"So, what's so important that my little brother felt the need to drag me and my family out of bed at daybreak?" Crystal Parker asked her mother, as she ushered her brood across the threshold. "And why are you answering the door? Where's Caleb?"

"First of all, young lady, stop being so dramatic," Claudia Campbell replied. "It's not daybreak. It's a bit later than that. But, to answer your question, it's a mystery to me too, but whatever your brother has in store involves that window right over there. And, he had to step out. He should be getting here a little later."

"Well, whatever it is, it'd better be good," Caleb's brother-in-law Ken said. "I'm missing my 8:00 tee time for this."

"I'm sure it will be well worth it," Claudia Campbell replied. She turned to her daughter. "And, by the way, where's your other brother?"

"Christian's parking his car, Mom," Crystal replied. "I'm sure he'll be up in a couple of minutes."

"Did someone just call my name!?" Christian Campbell bellowed. He shed his jacket upon entering his brother's space.

"Uncle Chris!" Caleb's niece and nephew shrieked. Christian Campbell squatted just in time to receive bear hugs.

"There, there now," Claudia Campbell said. "Release your uncle, please because we don't have much time. Now, y'all go and grab your binoculars. They should be labeled with your names. Your uncle Caleb wants us to each take a pair and get ready to look out that there window at eight o'clock sharp!"

"Okay," Christian Campbell said. "Where's mine? This had better be good—wakin' me outta my sleep at darn near the crack of dawn."

"My sentiments exactly," Crystal Parker said.

"Now, y'all hush up now," Claudia Campbell replied. "It's almost time. Now, go on over to the window."

They each raised their binoculars at exactly 8:00 a.m. and aimed them across the field and then over the hill as instructed. They adjusted the devices until the large banyan tree came into view. They panned them down to the base of the tree where four small squirrels huddled expectantly in a circle. Their tiny heads and tails took turns bobbing up and down in anticipation. A few feet away from them perched their bushy tailed mother, nearly twice their size. The animal turned away from them and faced the street on the tree's opposite side. It twitched and jerked quickly before it sprinted across the road just before oncoming traffic overtook the tarred pavement. The creature then scampered towards the large oak tree whose outer roots had begun to crack the pavement about fifty feet from the road's edge. The creature lifted an acorn from the bed of several that lay at the base of the tree. The squirrel then dashed back across the street in an instant. It dropped the acorn at the feet of its offspring before turning back toward the road in preparation to repeat the process.

"Wow!" the Parker issue exclaimed. "All that work to get one acorn!"

"Yep," Claudia Campbell said. "And I bet she'll keep going until she gets enough for each of her little ones."

Approximately fifteen minutes passed before the large squirrel completed her task, with an acorn resting at the feet of all of her offspring. Each lifted its acorn before scurrying up the banyan tree. Only after they reached their destination within the uppermost branches did the large squirrel scamper up to join them.

"Well, what I don't get is why the big one didn't just go and bring a whole bunch of acorns back so it doesn't have to go back and forth so much," Ken Parker said. "You know, stock up."

"Well, I think I know why," Crystal Parker replied. "Look over there past the tree on the other side of the street."

Everyone steered their binoculars as instructed until several other large squirrels came into view. Each one arriving at the base of the tree to remove one acorn at a time.

"Now, do you see?" Claudia Campbell asked.

"Ah, yes," they all replied.

"I totally get it," Caleb's nephew said.

"Cool!" Caleb's niece exclaimed.

"So, who wants to come downstairs with me?" Christian Campbell asked. "I got some gifts in my trunk for a couple of kids I heard have been really good this year."

"In a few minutes, Uncle Chris," Caleb's nephew said.

"We wanna finish watching this," Caleb's niece added.

Caleb's mother redirected her binoculars away from the trees and toward the courtyard beneath the windowsill to find her son staring up at her. She lowered her binoculars, lifted her right hand and thumb so her son could see. He smiled.

TWO GOOD EGGS

"Hey, why can't you be more like your brother?" Kelvin's dad shouted before giving all his attention to the TV screen that projected the image of his other son scoring yet another touchdown en route to a playoff victory that would cement his team's place in the high school championship game three weeks later. From Dad's perspective, the fact that the city had begun to broadcast his son's playoff games was like icing on an otherwise perfect seven-layer cake of a football season. "You could learn a lot from him, you know."

Realizing his dad did not really require a response to the question he asked, Kelvin remained seated at the kitchen table and continued to scribble, erase, then scribble some more, determined to solve the scientific riddle that glared at him from the white parchment on the table below him. The words and numbers dared him to do what many others had attempted, but failed. Kelvin had barely slept the previous night as the images and formulas in his brain took hold of his consciousness like a vise. Kelvin hoped the notes he had penned during those early morning hours, when the mental tossing and turning compelled him to write, would prove helpful. He sat at the kitchen table convinced he was on the verge of a breakthrough.

The momentary interruption brought on by his dad's voice did allow Kelvin to shift his focus for a moment, however. He pondered how ridiculously accurate the observation underlying his dad's question was. It was true that he and his brother were born on the same date and, indeed, shared the same womb for nine months, ten days and three minutes. But it was also true that he and his brother, despite their identical physical appearances, in many respects seemed as different as night and day. Kristoff played football. Kelvin loved chess. Kristoff listened to hip hop. Kelvin preferred jazz. Kristoff watched "Supermarket Sweep" and "WWE Smackdown." Kelvin preferred "Jeopardy" and the Discovery channel. There could be no denying that they were two very different peas living in the same pod. To Kelvin, it seemed that no matter what he did, his Dad would always prefer one pea over the other.

The hour and a half that elapsed while Kelvin sat at the kitchen table completely engrossed in his formula would have gone completely unnoticed were it not for Mom's voice.

"Kelvin, please eat your breakfast before it gets cold," Mom implored, as Kelvin continued to rack his brain. "You can finish that later."

"Mom, I'm on a roll here," Kelvin replied. "Give me a couple of minutes."

"Okay, but you are not to leave this table until you finish, do you understand?" Mom asked.

"Yes, ma'am," Kelvin replied. He craned his neck briefly toward the plate of food. "Hey, you didn't give me any eggs? You know I'm trying to keep my protein levels high, Mom. It helps keep my mind clear."

"Yes, sir," Mom said. She opened the refrigerator door to retrieve the carton of eggs. "I'm just happy to hear you say you want something to eat at all—one side of eggs coming right up."

The odor that leapt from the carton of eggs as Mom removed them from the refrigerator attacked Kelvin's nostrils with a vengeance. His left hand instinctively released his pencil and made an immediate beeline to join his right hand that already covered his nose and mouth.

"What is that awful smell?" Kelvin mumbled through interlaced fingers.

"Looks like the eggs have gone bad," Mom replied. "Not to worry, though. I bought another carton yesterday. They're in the back of the fridge. First, let me go outside and throw these...."

As Mom said this, Kelvin looked down at his notes, grabbed Mom's free hand and exclaimed.

"That's it! No, wait! Don't throw them out. I need them."

"What in the world are you talking about?" Mom asked.

"I need them for my project," Kelvin replied.

"Whatever for?" Mom asked.

"What in the world is that foul odor?" Dad asked as he entered the kitchen from the den where he'd been watching Kristoff's football game.

"It's the sulfur from the eggs, Dad!" Kelvin exclaimed, smiling like a Cheshire cat. He lifted the carton. "This is the bomb diggity, Dad!"

"Yeah, if you say so, son," Dad replied, staring blankly at his wife.

"Gotta go!" Kelvin shouted. He scooped up the notes and books that were scattered about the table into his arms, shoved them into his back pack and sprinted from the kitchen toward the front door.

Dad watched him exit the kitchen, then turned to Mom and twirled his index finger in a circular motion next to his ear.

"It's official, he's lost it," Dad said.

"What about your breakfast?" Mom yelled toward the front door. She swatted Dad's hand away from his ear.

"I'll eat it later!" Kelvin replied, as the front door behind him began to close.

"And what about the eggs?" Mom asked.

"Don't need them after all, Mom," Kelvin answered. He aimed a finger from his free hand towards his head. "I've got what I need right up here."

"Oh, well," Dad said to Mom. "There goes your son. Sometimes I think that boy needs some serious help."

"Now, that's enough, Max," Mom said. "He's just a different boy. You really should make an effort to get to know him better."

"Um, yeah, that's gonna happen," Dad replied. He reached down and grabbed an uneaten slice of toast from his son's plate and took a bite.

"By the way," Dad continued. "Your *other* son just scored three touchdowns this morning."

"He did?" Mom replied. "That's great news, dear."

"Great? It's the bomb diggity!" Dad exclaimed.

"I'm proud of him too, Max," Mom replied. "Just try not to forget you have two sons!"

"Yeah, yeah," Dad said before exiting the kitchen.

Ensuring her sons knew she loved and supported them equally had been of paramount importance to Mom since the time the boys were little. From the time she knew she was having twins, Mom made an effort to study the leading publications discussing the unique challenges associated with rearing them. She paid particular attention to those that focused on the long-lasting effects of favoring one twin over the other. For this reason, she made it her personal mission to take action to ensure they received equal time when it came to the attention she showered on them.

As nine-year-old Kristoff scored his first six shots in a row during his first pee-wee basketball game on the neighborhood court while a crowd of onlookers cheered him on (from a young age, Kristoff had excelled at most sports), she made sure to offer encouragement to nine-year-old Kelvin as he solved advanced geometrical theorems and postulates one after the other while crouched over his steno pad in the bleachers. If no one else appreciated the value in her other son's mental gifts, she knew she would. So, while she and Dad cheered like the other parents in appreciation of Kristoff's athletic prowess, with each basket Kristoff made, she gently stroked the back of Kelvin's head and whispered in his ear.

"Good job, son."

Having just left the kitchen, Dad ascended the staircase, glanced to the right and observed the framed photos of family and friends that had accumulated over the years until his eyes fixated on one. There it was—the picture of him, Mom, and his two sons. It was taken when the boys were nine, the day of Kristoff's first pee-wee basketball game. At the end of the game, Wanda Perkins, their next-door neighbor, had asked for a picture of the star player's entire family. Brimming with pride, Dad could not help but oblige, so he summoned Mom and Kelvin from the bleachers and positioned the two boys in front of him and Mom. He asked Kelvin to lower his steno pad and pencil for a moment and then positioned Mom to his right.

"Wow, Max, I never realized the boys really do look exactly the same," Wanda said while staring at the boys. At that moment, they both instinctively and simultaneously took their right hands and smoothed the hair that had fallen into their eyes to the left of their foreheads, faced each other and smiled.

"Okay, on the count of three, I want you all to smile," Wanda continued. "Not just the boys, all of you."

"You got it," Dad replied.

"Here we go," Wanda said. "One, two, three."

Dad could not remember the flash from the camera, but he could remember with great clarity the image of Wanda's husband Troy standing behind and to the left of Wanda as she snapped the photo—the image of Troy pointing at the steno pad and pencil in Kelvin's left hand while laughing and whispering something into the ear of the person standing next to him. The urge to punch Troy for laughing at his son as he pulled Kelvin a bit closer also flooded Dad's memory, causing the hair on the back of his neck to stand on end. Dad had always wondered what Troy whispered.

Dad diverted his eyes from the photo, shook his head and continued up the staircase and entered his bedroom for a much-needed nap.

"Bruh, I heard you were great out there today," Kelvin said to his brother when he entered Kristoff's bedroom to give him a congratulatory fist bump.

"Yeah, but they were pretty tough out there today," Kristoff replied. He stared at his computer screen and continued to breeze through his calculus homework. "Now, it's all about the state championship in three weeks. That game's gonna be a war."

"You'll be ready for it," Kelvin replied, while making one, and only one, correction to his brother's math homework. The rest of his work, as usual, was perfect."

"We'll see," Kristoff said. "I just hope the weather finally cools off. This eighty-degree weather in December is really starting to get old."

"Speaking of the weather...," Kelvin said. He smiled at his brother and began to turn to exit his bedroom.

"What?" Kristoff replied. "Are you kidding me!? You finally figured it out?"

Kelvin turned his head back toward his brother and winked.

"We go live in about three weeks."

He stepped out of his brother's bedroom and closed the door behind him.

Kristoff smiled and turned back toward his computer. With two clicks of his mouse, he accessed the file containing the advanced climate control databank his brother had sent him several days earlier. He began to open the file to review the most recent formulas he hoped his brother already had uploaded into the file when he heard a knock at the door.

"Hey, son!" Dad yelled. "Good stuff out there today. Got a few minutes to give your old man the play by play?"

"Sure, Dad," Kristoff replied. "Just gimme a second."

Kristoff closed the climate control data file, changed the television channel to sports, and raised the volume. He opened his bedroom door.

"Hey, Dad," Kristoff said. "Come on in."

* * *

The day of the high school state championship football game was a blustery eighty-four degrees Fahrenheit. The heat index made it feel like ninety-four. The day was completely unlike the thirteen others that preceded it in terms of temperature. There really was nothing terribly unusual about the day in that regard. The only unusual thing about the day, like the thirteen others that preceded it, was that it happened to fall during the month of December. Granted, if the temperature gauge had read *eighty-four* in Miami, no one would have given it a second thought. The fact that such a temperature was being recorded in Seattle had caused more than a few people to become a bit concerned.

"It's that damned global warming, I tell ya," insisted Joanne Crabtree, as she shepherded her two grandchildren into the stadium bleachers in the row behind Mom and Dad to secure prime seating before the big game.

"I don't believe in that personally," replied Tucker Wilson, Dad's golf buddy, who sat in the row in front of Joanne and next to Mom and Dad. He turned back toward the field to face the American flag and removed his hat in anticipation of the National Anthem. "It's just something them lefties came up with to justify more government spending on crap research and science we don't need."

Mom and Dad stared at Tucker, looked at each other and shook their heads. They had become accustomed to holding their tongues in the face of such statements in one of the few conservative enclaves in the otherwise progressive city they called home for the better part of three years, an unexpected relocation that came at the expense of his wife's major job promotion.

Kristoff and his fellow teammates huddled in front of the large fan on the sidelines while Coach Patton shouted last minute instructions before game time. Kristoff craned his neck to the right to catch a glimpse of Mom and Dad in the stands and acknowledged them both with a nod. They returned the gesture. Kristoff scanned the rows to the right and to the left of his parents but did not see his brother anywhere.

As the first half of the game came to a close and the final seconds ticked off the game clock, Kristoff sprinted to the sideline in anticipation of grabbing a much-needed breather. After all, he had single-handedly scored the team's only two touchdowns of the half, the more thrilling of which, an eighty-two-yard run, coming just two minutes before the end of the half.

"You want me to grab a hand-held fan for ya, Kris?" Assistant Coach Johnson asked as he motioned for one of the student assistants.

"No, sir," Kristoff answered. "No need. I'm fine. I just need to sit down for a few minutes. Is it me or did it just get cooler all of a sudden?"

"You know, you're right," Assistant Coach Johnson replied. "It's almost cool enough for me to run to the car to get my windbreaker. And it sure is dark for four in the afternoon. I'm surprised they haven't turned on the stadium lights."

As Assistant Coach Johnson said this, a student assistant draped a towel around Kristoff's shoulders. Kristoff turned to the stands to get a reassuring nod from Mom and Dad. Still no sign of his brother. Kristoff wondered where he could be. With each degree the temperature dropped, a look of knowing excitement crept across Kristoff's face. He smiled. He knew why his brother was not at the game.

As the ten-minute halftime clock ticked off its last seconds to signal the commencement of the second half, Annie Wilson, Tucker Wilson's wife, held up her smartphone screen and exclaimed.

"Hey, Max, isn't that your son, Kelvin?"

Dad reached over to grab the device and peered at its screen, pulling it in closely so both he and Mom could watch. The device was live streaming from the Weather Channel. Two men who appeared to be around Dad's age sat behind a makeshift desk that was positioned outdoors in such a way as to have Mount Rainier and its missing snowcap in the background. There also appeared to be an extremely long cylindrical contraption with large globes attached to it that extended into the sky behind them. Between the two men sat a teenage boy whose lips were moving.

"Annie, can you pass us your earbuds, please?" Dad asked.

"Sorry about that, Max," Annie replied. "Here you go."

"Thanks," Dad replied.

He positioned one of the ear buds over his lobe and handed the other to Mom, who immediately did the same. The sound burst through the earbuds and there was no mistaking that Mom and Dad were listening to and looking at their son.

The referee blew the whistle to start the second half. Mom and Dad continued to stare at Annie's smartphone screen, transfixed by the images and sounds that emanated from the device.

"Most scientists have been attempting to solve the climate change issue primarily through a reduction in carbon emissions," Kelvin said to the interviewer. "This solution is all well and good. It's always a good practice for human beings to reduce their carbon footprint. The trouble with that approach is that the benefits of it, assuming all nations across the globe agree to take immediate steps to employ that method, will not be felt for many years. That's when we began to brainstorm. What if we could think outside the box and devise a method that could affect the global warming phenomenon immediately? After many months of study, it finally hit me."

"When did it, as you say, hit you?" the interviewer asked.

"About three weeks ago actually," Kelvin replied. "And in the most bizarre of all places. My mom's kitchen."

Mom and Dad turned toward each other with mouths wide open, hardly able to believe what their son was saying.

Kelvin proceeded to explain to the interviewer the rotten egg story and how that triggered within him the idea of projecting sulfur dioxide into the upper regions of the atmosphere with what he described as a massive cylindrical pump that would be transported via very large aircraft. He detailed the manner in which the sulfur dioxide captures and diverts the sun's rays to create an overcast atmosphere which necessarily would block the sun causing the temperature to fall. He gestured toward the contraption behind him and thanked the interviewer and other reporters for accompanying him and the rest of his colleagues in what he described as a test run.

The crowd jumped and screamed around Dad as six more points appeared on the scoreboard. Kristoff's teammates lifted him to their shoulders seconds later after he crossed the goal line for the third time. There was no doubt that his team was en route to certain victory. Dad remained anchored to his seat. He draped his arm around Mom in an effort to shield her from the cooling air. He smiled and continued to stare at Kelvin's image on the small screen.

"Now that's the bomb diggity," he said to Mom. She nodded her head in agreement.

HOPE

GREENY'S GAMBLE

Greeny basked in the searing South Florida sunshine while straddling the long embankment separating the forty-two-story concrete cube to his left from the bay's undulating ripples to his right. The dearth of four-wheelers that typically traversed the high-arching roadway he faced signaled something was different. But he couldn't quite put his scaly foot pad on it.

"Man, I forgot how hot it could get out here!" the tinny-voice hissed. The gecko from which it came flicked his long tongue from right eye to left for moisture. "That sun's blazing!"

"Yeah, it's great, right?" Greeny replied. He surveyed the creature from tip to tail. "Um, I hope you don't get offended when I say this, but from where I sit, it sure looks like you need it!"

"No offense taken." The gecko inclined his head toward the condominium tower. "I got booted from my place during mid-molt. No warning, no nothing. So, please excuse my appearance."

"Well, that sucks," Greeny replied. The embankment began to swell with an unusually large number of his distant mini-reptilian kin. "But I will say it's great to see you guys again."

"You too, man," the gecko said. "And I think you probably should get ready to see a lot more of us. For some reason, more and more of the two-leggers are staying inside the concrete cube these days. And, when I say *staying*, I mean all day, every day."

"Really?" Greeny asked.

"Yep," the gecko replied. "And that means they want us out."

"How strange," Greeny said.

"Isn't it?" the gecko whispered. "And despite what you see here, all of us don't make it out alive."

"The great splat?" Greeny asked.

"Yep," the gecko replied. "I'm just thankful my two-leggers were more compassionate. They scooped me off the wall, brought me down and left me by the pool."

"I couldn't help but overhear, and I agree something weird's going on," the baritone-voiced, brownish-green iguana to Greeny's rear announced. It was his old buddy, Ronny. "My cousin crossed the street last week."

A hush fell over the embankment.

"We're sorry for your loss, man," Greeny said.

"What loss?" Ronny replied. "She made it across and back again."

News of the occurrence spread like wildfire. Greeny closed his eyes. He recalled his grandmother's stories of his ancestors' worry-free movement across all parts without fear of the great splat. He'd believed the time for such indulgences had long passed, especially with the invasion of ever-present four-wheelers and the ubiquitous concrete cubes from which they often emerged. But, in recent days he'd noticed the concrete cubes trapped most of the four-wheelers inside. His grandmother often spoke of a second coming—a time when his kind could roam again without fear of the great splat. Greeny opened his eyes and counted a full fifteen seconds before he saw one, and *only* one, four-wheeler speed across the massive streetscape that soared over the water and connected the land mass on which he sat to that situated to his East.

Upon returning from his trip down memory lane, Greeny noticed his friends had vanished. He turned around, his long tail spilling over the lip of the embankment. In the distance, he saw they'd glommed onto an increasingly large group that surrounded a striking emerald colored beauty. She spoke from a position elevated above the rest. Greeny traversed the length of the embankment in a flash. He crouched next to Ronny in the back of the crowd before stretching upward. He inclined his head to the right so he could hear.

"Yes, my friends!" Ronny's cousin shouted. "The sun was definitely out when it happened. Kind of like today. It was not under cover of night."

"So, were all the four-wheelers gone when it happened?" someone asked.

"No, they weren't," she replied. "They were out. Just not nearly as many. That means, when you go—"

Whispers swept across those assembled.

"No, your ears don't deceive you, my friends," Ronny's cousin continued. "I did say *when* you go, because I firmly believe you all should go. It is *our* time! But you've got to be cautious because some of them still want to do us harm. We all know the type. The ones who find us on sidewalks sleeping on cool nights after the torpor topple, then cage us or sell us or..."

"Cook and eat us!" someone shouted.

Gasps and groans erupted, followed by a moment of silence.

"Yes, cook and eat us!" Ronny's cousin exclaimed. "So, we have to be vigilant. But I am living proof that it can be done. And I'm doing it again tomorrow. My cousin Ronny's coming with me and I hope you will too."

Ronny's eyes bulged. His dewlap ballooned to its capacity. He swallowed hard, then turned toward Greeny.

"You coming with us, buddy?"

"I, um, guess," Greeny stuttered. "We're gonna die *someday*, right?"

"Amen, brother," Ronny replied.

***

Greeny awoke early the next morning and met his friends at the only corner where dandelions still cracked pavement. He craned his head upward to see a group of wild parrots loudly holding court among the branches of the banyan, confident descendants of the once-confined aviators that were freed twenty-eight years prior by the winds of Hurricane Andrew. Rapid wing flaps accompanied their shrieks of encouragement. Ronny's cousin stepped forward first. Greeny followed, gingerly easing one footpad into the street, then the other. He sighed heavily before commencing his trek across the road's wide expanse.

He'd barely reached its midpoint when he spied in the distance a four-wheeler careening towards them. As his compatriots proceeded with their march, Greeny paused and weighed the odds of survival if he were to turn back. Then, he heard it—the extended screech of the four-wheeler that froze a few feet from the group. It waited as Greeny and his friends continued their side-to-side strut across the street until they reached their destination on the other side.

THE HERO, THE HEALER, AND HARVEY

August 25, 2017
"Grab my arm!" the dark-hued man exclaimed, his forearm seamlessly slicing the charging water like a hot knife through butter.

"But, my pa," Cooter replied. He steered his tear-swelled eyes away from the man and back toward the home that had sheltered him during his entire ten years of existence. He fixed his eyes upon the structure in a futile attempt to will any sign of life to exit. His hands clung to the uppermost branch of the old oak tree that stubbornly anchored itself to the ground in the middle of the flooded front yard of the Calhoun property. Cooter and his friends had frolicked freely in the same yard, rounding the trunk of the same tree a mere two days prior. The tree had been the focal point of the sprawling, two-acre tract of land that had been in Cooter's family for generations.

During countless springs, its leaves had fanned outward to shield Cooter and his friends from the sun's unrelenting rays as they played tag, hid and sought, hunted for colored eggs. In the fall, the same leaves had browned and fallen in bunches to become the bounteous backdrop for his family's annual Halloween boo bash celebrations. How fitting it was that the tree would serve as the family's dependable port in the midst of the historic storm that threatened to drown hundreds of homes in the exclusive, blue blood enclave along the outskirts of metropolitan Houston. Steadfast, reliable, and strong, now as then, the oak took great pains to provide support on yet another occasion as the youngling that had frequently and happily scaled its branches now clasped its highest extremities with an anguished look of concern.

"The water's almost up to your neck now!" the man exclaimed. "Take my hand before it's too late!"

"I can't leave here without my pa," the boy replied. He looked past the man in the boat to catch a glimpse of a familiar face that sat stock-still in the water-soaked seat behind him.

"Your pa, um, told me to come get you while he makes, um, final preparations to secure the house!" the man lied, the circumstances of the moment compelling him to spin any tale he could to compel the boy to make the right decision. The truth was the man had never met Cooter's dad and, under the circumstances, never would.

"My pa ain't told you that!" Cooter sneered. "He don't got no nigger friends, so you best be goin' now! Go on! Git!"

The man paused briefly to consider the venom that spewed from Cooter's lips as easily as the boy breathed. The man began to remove his outstretched hand from the water. The beginnings of a smile appeared on the face of the boy sitting behind the man when he saw his father's arm continue to recoil and move away from Cooter. His smile vanished quickly, however, upon seeing instinct compel his father to lift and extend both his arms swiftly to rip Cooter from the tree he hugged moments before the swells consumed Cooter completely.

"Now, get inside this boat before you die!" the man yelled. He tossed Cooter's seventy-five-pound frame into the boat. It landed next to his son's. Cooter cried mightily, his eyes firmly affixed upon the house he grew up in, which grew smaller and smaller as the boat sped away.

"Now, keep your eyes open for any other stragglers!" the man shouted to his son.

"I will, Daddy," his son replied. He glared stoically at their vessel's newest occupant.

* * *

"Any parents?" the elder asked. He stared in Cooter's general direction.

"No, Imam," the man replied. "Just the boy. And I should tell you, Imam…"

"Yes?" the elder asked.

"I strongly believe his parents may not have made it."

"What makes you say that?" the elder asked.

"The boy told us he was waiting for his father when we found him," the man replied. "And, at that point, the water was already beginning to cover the roof of his house."

"Oh, no," the elder said.

"Yes, it didn't look good at all, Imam," the man replied.

"Well, we need to contact the police and fire departments right away," the elder said.

"Yes, Imam," the man replied. "We did so as soon as we arrived here at the mosque."

"Good," the elder aid. "No need to assume the worst. Let's just wait to see what law enforcement comes back with."

"Agreed," the man replied. "And in the meantime? What do we tell the boy? He's been asking about his 'pa' since the time we picked him up."

"Well," the elder began, "Allah will show us the way with him. Meanwhile, we just have to find ways to keep him engaged and occupied. Tariq is around his age, is he not?"

"I believe he is," the man replied. "But, for whatever reason, from the moment we picked the boy up, Tariq has kept his distance from him. And I'm not sure why."

"Hmm," the elder said. "Do you want me to talk to Tariq?"
"Yes, Imam," the man replied. "You've always had a way with him."

***

August 21, 2017
"Tanaka, Mufasa, Boofasa!" the wiry, strawberry blond-haired boy exclaimed. His makeshift band of brothers, more than fifteen in number, doubled over in laughter upon hearing him as Tariq cowered in the corner. "Tell us your name again!"

"Leave me alone!" Tariq implored.

"Or is it Chewbacca?" another boy, smaller than the rest, shouted from the back of the pack. The boys guffawed loudly and with even more intensity like a pack of hyenas. "After all, they *are* the same color!"

The swell of humanity that stood before him began to part slightly. Tariq caught a glimpse of the crimson-colored hair that crowned the head of the person who lobbed the most crushing insult against him to date. Then, he heard a voice.

"Cooter Calhoun!" the teacher exclaimed. "Did I just hear you call a fellow classmate by something other than his name?"

"Yes, ma'am," Cooter replied. "I said it. My pa says these terrorist niggers got no business being in our school anyway!"

"Well, your pa is wrong!" the teacher exclaimed, the fury in her voice manifesting itself in the beet red color that began to spread across the surface of her otherwise paper-white skin. "And I'll tell him so the next time I see him! Racist comments and bullying have no place in this school. You hear me? We are all about tolerance here, young man. Nobody's better than anybody else. And the fact that somebody has a different skin color than you doesn't mean they don't deserve the same respect as you. Now, you gather your things right this instant and go down to the principal's office so you can think about what I just said!"

Tariq watched Cooter Calhoun stomp down the hallway, then collected his books and other belongings that minutes earlier had been knocked to the ground. Tariq paused and lowered his head for thirty seconds, before sprinting to the restroom at the end of the fourth-grade hallway of the ultra-exclusive Treadwell Friends Academy in the Waverly Wings subdivision of western Houston.

***

"Tariq Ibrahim Mustafa," the elder began. He folded himself into the chair abutting the young man's cot before tapping Tariq gently on his back. "How long have we known each other?"

"Ever since I was born, Imam," Tariq replied.

"No, Tariq," the elder said. "Even longer. I've known you since you were a little pea in your mother's pod. And, you know, since the time you formed your first words and could really understand mine, I've always told you there's nothing you can't talk to me about, haven't I?"

"You have, Imam," Tariq replied.

"So, talk to me, Tariq," the elder said. He gazed at the red-headed boy who sat on the opposite side of the auditorium. "Your father tells me you don't like that boy. What is happening with you that you cannot show him a little kindness, especially now when Allah is testing him and all of us so?"

"I don't know," Tariq lied.

"Okay," the elder said. "Well, can you at least do me one small favor?"

"Sure," Tariq replied. "What is it, Imam?"

"Can you try, Tariq?" the elder asked. "After all, unlike you, who Allah has decided to spare extreme heartache in his latest test of nature's fury, I believe this boy may not have been so blessed. I think he may have lost his parents."

"Really, Imam?" Tariq said.

"Yes, Tariq," the elder replied. "It's not confirmed yet, but I believe they may not have survived."

"Oh, no!" Tariq exclaimed. Tears began to stream down his cheeks.

"Tariq," the elder began. "It will be okay. We have resources here at the mosque to help him. In the end, he will be okay. But, it's up to all of us to help him."

Two full minutes elapsed before Tariq interrupted the silence that hovered between them.

"I did it, Imam," Tariq said, between sobs. "It's all my fault."

"What are you talking about, Tariq?" the elder replied. "What's your fault?"

"I killed his parents, Imam," Tariq said. "After he and the other boys pushed me at school and called me the 'n-word,' I prayed and prayed for Allah to hurt all of them badly—just as badly as they hurt me. That's why his parents died, Imam. I know it! I killed them!"

"Tariq, Tariq, calm down," the elder replied. "You did no such thing. It is not for us to know why Allah does what He does."

"It isn't, Imam?" Tariq asked.

"No, Tariq," the elder replied. "It isn't. What is important for us to know is that no matter what circumstance Allah places us in, we have a solemn duty to Allah to look out for one another, and many times that means forgiving one another for the bad things we sometimes do to each other, even when that feels like the most difficult thing in the world to do."

"So, you think I should forgive him for what he did and said to me?" Tariq asked.

"Yes, I know you should," the elder replied. "And I also know something else."

"What, Imam?" Tariq asked.

"I also know you should stop beating yourself up and forgive yourself, Tariq," the elder replied. "For wishing bad things to happen to the boy after he hurt you. You know why?"

"Why, Imam?" Tariq asked.

"Because the biggest weapon you can launch against hatred—even self-hatred—is not more hatred."

"It isn't, Imam?" Tariq asked.

"No, it is not, Tariq," the elder replied. "The biggest weapon against hatred is love."

"It is?" Tariq asked.

"Yes, it is," the elder said. "Because hatred feeds off hatred and only grows and gets stronger, but hatred does not know how to react in the face of love. Eventually, it has no other choice but to go away and disappear."

Tariq sat with the elder for ten minutes more, during which time the elder peppered him gently with more questions about Cooter Calhoun, his school and its reaction and response to Tariq's encounter. Tariq then allowed his tear-stained eyes to rest upon Cooter Calhoun, who sat by himself on the pallet of quilts and blanket that were assembled for him in the corner of the mosque's 3,500-square-foot basement.

"So, you think I should go talk to him, Imam?" Tariq asked.

"I think you should," the elder replied. "He looks pretty lonely. And, Tariq, don't be discouraged if he doesn't warm up to you right away. Remember, a lot has happened to him over the past couple of days."

* * *

"So, how did it go with Tariq, Imam?" the man asked.

"It went fine," the elder replied. "I think he's going to be okay."

"So, what's going on with him?" the man asked.

"Now, you know that's between the two of us," the elder replied, laughing. "Just take comfort in knowing your son is growing up to be a fine Muslim. And, as for the boy you brought in the other day…."

"Yes, Imam?" the man asked. "What about him?"

"Let's just say I'm glad you brought him to us when you did," the elder replied.

"Well, this was the first place I thought to go, Imam," the man said. "You and I both know this mosque has been the shelter in many a storm in my life, so it was a no-brainer for me—even with our recent move to the 'burbs. Besides, who would have thought most of the would-be shelters in the 'well to do' sections of the city would suffer the level of flooding they did? Interesting, isn't it, that our not-so-little mosque on the other side of the tracks has become one of the last best options for many newly homeless Houstonians?'"

"Indeed, it is," the elder replied. "And, as for the boy, after the trauma he's experienced, both recent and not-so-recent, he's going to need a lot of help, more than you and I realize. And, until anyone comes to claim him, this is just the place to provide it."

* * *

August 30, 2023
"So, you're saying the sellers are asking just five hundred thousand dollars for all this land *and* this house?" the husband-to-be asked.

The realtor's self-driving electric sedan steered itself into the driveway of the property and slowly came to a stop, as the couple that accompanied him surveyed the property.

"Yes," the realtor replied. "The property is being held in trust for a young man who is not quite old enough to make his own decisions. And, the executor of his father's estate was given specific instructions to try to sell when the boy turned sixteen, and then use the proceeds to fund his higher education."

"You don't say," the husband-to-be said.

"Yes, sir," the realtor replied. "As you can see, the home has sustained significant damage. That was caused by Hurricane Harvey years ago when virtually the entire neighborhood was flooded. It's only gotten worse over the years from lack of repair and maintenance. But the house can be razed. Maybe you could start from scratch?"

"And what about this large stump in the middle of the yard?" the wife-to-be asked. She exited the vehicle, pointing at the rotted wood that protruded partially from the ground.

"Well, that's a bit of a sad story in itself," the realtor replied. "That was an oak tree, one that stood firm for more than a hundred years on this property. For several days after Harvey, it held, but over time, like so much of this neighborhood, it, too, perished. It's a shame really."

The wife-to-be turned to the husband-to-be.

"Well, I've already got some ideas swirling about what to grow there," she said. "After that stump is uprooted completely, that is."

"So, does that mean you want to make an offer?" the realtor asked.

The husband-to-be looked at his fiancée and smiled.

"Did you notice, babe?" he asked. "It faces East. Perfect for prayers."

The wife-to-be turned to the realtor.

"Please forgive my fiancé for his rudeness. He did not answer your question, but I will. Yes, we want to make an offer."

VESTIGES

Until then, the background had been Noah's preferred residence in virtually every circumstance involving a spotlight or crowd. Ever saddled with the baggage that often accompanied his frequent journeys to the front of the line, the classroom, the stage, the struggle was real. Not that most would notice.

"You got this!" Katrina Washington shrieked, breaking Noah's train of thought for a moment.

Audible hisses rippled throughout the middle school auditorium, underscoring the audience's general disapproval of his sister's breach of decorum. Noah smiled, took a deep breath. He glanced to his left, noting the countdown clock on the wall. Forty-five seconds left. He lifted his left hand, palm facing up. His right index finger did the rest, tickling his left palm with familiar rapid strokes to form the letters. He dropped both hands, lowered his head and closed his eyes. Fresh memories of tirades blunting his mother's defense of her son's decision to forego athletic team sports to free up time for more scholarly pursuits flooded his mind. His dad had been ferocious in his attacks. Noah shook his head to push the memories aside. A second deep breath escaped his lips. His eyelids parted bringing into view the microphone before him.

"Intransigent," Noah said. "I-N-T-R-A-N-S-I-G-E-N-T. Intransigent?"

Three seconds elapsed with no discernible ring to signal his etymological demise.

"Correct," the judge said.

Noah sighed, swept perspiration from his brow with his spelling hand and returned to his seat. The moment he folded himself into his chair, applause filled the room. Unlike the shushes that quelled his sister's outburst moments earlier, noise flowed freely throughout the auditorium's airspace for the entire sixty seconds it took for Amanda Morrissey to stride confidently toward the microphone. She eyed Noah with contempt before facing the audience and the competition judge. With each round of the Bee, Noah sensed Amanda's surprise as their contemporaries fell victim to the sting of the bell one by one until only she and Noah remained. The others, like Amanda, had consistently occupied the upper echelons of the school's academic hierarchy, receiving one accolade after another for their myriad achievements. While Noah had shared space among them in the Advanced Placement classes reserved for the school's intellectual elite, he typically would position himself comfortably in the least conspicuous sections of those spaces. The rear of the class, the end of the line. Yet, here he was. Out front. One of two students left to slug it out in the gladiators' circle. Noah turned his head away from his adversary as she commenced her queries that would assist in her assessment of how to arrange her letters. Instead, Noah cast his gaze upon the freshly waxed flooring beneath him, hoping to hasten the exodus of the metaphorical butterflies that continued to harass his insides. In the ensuing moments it took for his competitor to spell her word successfully, he recalled his mother's candor following the weeks it took her to convince her husband that her support for her son's decision had not been misplaced.

***

"Now that I've helped you win this battle, I want something in return, Noah," she had said. "Because I figure you do owe me one."

"Yes, Ma'am," Noah had replied.

"I need you to promise me that you won't make a fool of me," she had said. She'd moved strands of hair from behind her ear towards her face to conceal remnants of the recently acquired bruise she received on his behalf.

"I won't," Noah had replied.

"I mean it, Noah," his mother had said. "I know that it's in your nature to shy away from the spotlight and taking the lead, but I'm here to tell you I'm not gon' always be here to intercede on your behalf."

"Ma'am?" Noah had asked.

"I know it's hard to hear, but it's true," his mother had replied. "So, I need you to promise me right here, right now, that when situations require it—and you'll know what I'm talking about when it happens—you will push past your natural urge to recede and that you will step forward, with confidence. I mean, I know you've got the goods up there."

She gestured towards his head.

"Okay," Noah had replied.

"After all," she had continued. "You're just as smart as those other kids at that school we're sending you to. Your grades show it. So, you have just as much right as they do to let it show and receive all the benefits and accomplishments for letting it show."

"Yes, Ma'am," Noah had replied.

"So, I need you to remember to always hold your head up," she had said. "And to not be afraid to let what I know is inside of you shine!"

***

Upon Amanda Morrissey's return to her seat, Noah lifted his head and stole a glance at the first row behind the competition judge. His mother's eyes met his before she nodded. He stood and commenced his thirty foot trek across the stage. He positioned himself behind the microphone for the eighteenth time and received his next word.

"May I have the definition, please?" he asked.

"A split or division between opposing sections or parties, caused by differences in opinion or belief," the judge replied.

"May I have the language of origin?" Noah asked.

"It is from the Latin 'schismat' and also from the Greek 'schizeim,' meaning to split," the judge replied.

Noah closed his eyes and took a deep breath. Images of his father storming past the threshold of the front door of his family's modest two-bedroom apartment with suitcase in hand competed with images of his younger sister's tear-stained face as she clung to their mother's waist. Guilt from his role in helping to expose the fissures in a relationship what was destined to end anchored Noah to the past. The loud cough and clearance of an adult's throat jolted him back to the present. He opened his eyes and caught a glimpse of his mother as she removed her cupped hand from her mouth. Noah glanced at the countdown clock, which displayed a scant ten seconds. He spelled.

"Schism," he said. "S-C-H-I-S-M. Schism?"

He paused the full three seconds before the words that would confirm he'd survived to move forward to the next round met his ears.

"That's correct," the judge said.

A momentary sigh of relief preceded his pilgrimage back towards temporary asylum. Light applause from the audience accompanied him. When Amanda Morrissey received her next word, she appeared perplexed. Noah smiled before closing his eyes and tilting his head upward. Images of his maternal grandmother grabbed his attention. Her presence in the Washington household had been a Godsend in the days following his father's exit. Her words were a much needed balm to soothe his and his sister's lingering wounds in those days.

***

"Now, I didn't leave the comfort of my home to come here and be a bump on the log for y'all," she had said. "We gon' have some fun around here, but then I'm gon' do some schoolin' to fill in the gaps left by them so-called teachers y'all have to deal with every day."

"So-called teachers, Ma-dear?" Noah had asked.

"You heard me, boy," his grandmother had replied. "I mean, I got nothin' against the formal schoolin' y'all getting from them. The math, the English, the science. But there some other things I know they ain't teachin' that is just as important that y'all need to know."

"Like what, Ma'dear?" Noah's sister asked.

"Well, if y'all gimme a minute, I'll tell you," Noah's grandmother had said. "Now, go fetch me that there book on top of my nightstand."

***

Amanda Morrissey had run out of the series of questions to which she was entitled as the time on the countdown clock dwindled. She sighed nervously into the microphone before she spoke.

"Diaspora," she said. "D-I-A-S-P-O-R-A-H. Diaspora?"

She flinched as the bell's ting, as if she'd just sustained a fresh cut to her person by an invisible assassin who'd swept across the stage without notice. The chime also sent Noah's heart racing, as he contemplated it was now within his power to seal his opponent's fate.

He lifted his frame from his seat and strode confidently towards the front of the stage without making eye contact with his schoolmate. He surveyed the sea of bodies that had assembled to witness which student would rise above the rest to become the school's sole representative at the Bee's district finals. Noah smiled briefly after the judge spoke. The wellspring of pride pouring from the row behind the judge rushed towards the stage, buoying Noah and providing him just the support he needed to carry him across the finish line.

"Metamorphosis," he said. "M-E-T-A-M-O-R-P-H-O-S-I-S. Metamorphosis?"

Five seconds elapsed before the judge spoke.

"Congratulations, Noah Washington, you are heading to the district finals!" the judge exclaimed.

Screams and applause flooded the auditorium hall. Arms raised, Noah smiled and directed his gaze towards the three generations of women whose moisture-tinged faces evidenced the release and relief of a family very much in need of a win.

A WOMAN'S WORTH

At times like these, the woman wonders what the point of it all is. Recent news of the unexpected death of yet another close friend, a mere two years her senior, came out of nowhere and rained down on her like a storm for which she was woefully unprepared. Sorrow cements her to the cream-colored recliner in her living room. She looks down. Her lap cradles the framed photo. Moisture wells just beneath the lower lip of her left eyelid. Knowing she must conserve the lion share of her sadness for the marathon day of grief lying in wait at her friend's funeral and burial, she rations just one tear. It eventually breaches the rim of her eyelid, journeys the length of her cheek and pools at the bottom of her chin. Then, gravity continues to have its way. The picture frame intercepts the liquid before it meets the ground. The woman wipes the droplet from the glass housing the most recent image of her dog Ozzie. Her furry friend had been gifted by her older brother fourteen years ago as a comfort in the wake of the untimely passing of her longtime human companion and soul mate of thirty-six years.

Lung cancer had been the thief that stole her husband. A short eight months from diagnosis to death. No time to prepare, as though there were any real way to do it. Without question, her husband's sudden passing had sucker-punched her, wounding her so deeply she was convinced she'd be out for the count. While not a complete cure for her ailment, Ozzie's arrival at her doorstep less than a year later eventually would prove to be a more than sufficient salve for her wound, especially in the absence of her adult children, with lives and families of their own.

Memories of a more vibrant, jet black pooch in those early days rush to the front of the woman's mind as she perceives every aspect of Ozzie's hunched over posture in the more recent photo she caresses. Ubiquitous bunches of coal colored fur had been replaced by salt-and-pepper strands at the neck line. She resists the urge to cry. Thoughts of the pain her dog surely endured in his final days compete with the joyous ones of the first time they met. Or are these thoughts of her husband?

"No, uh-uh," she murmurs to herself. "Can't do this right now."

She rests the picture on the table next to her recliner. She moves her freshly freed hands to her thighs. She gently begins to massage them. She extends her arms further down, repositioning her hands so that they cup her elevated ankles and feet, which rest atop the ottoman fronting her recliner.

"That's better," the woman says. She firmly kneads her flesh to facilitate circulation.

She notices the swelling that greeted her at dawn has diminished. She removes her hands momentarily. She raises her head. A photo housing an image of her younger version and her husband grabs her attention. It is perched atop the fireplace. On most days it would provoke a smile. On this day, it stops her in her tracks. It was taken in the seventies. He was dressed in his Navy uniform, she in a black and white polka dot dress. Her well-coiffed, ample Afro, like her husband, stands at attention. Her hands clasp his. The brightness of golden wedding bands and broad smiles compete for attention. The woman contemplates a smile, closes her eyes momentarily and recalls how she and her husband marveled at the prospect of the life that lay ahead of them. Thoughts of any life-threatening illness overtaking either of them were inconceivable. There was no thought of the lung cancer that would eventually take his life at the age of fifty-six, nor of the two replacement surgeries that would scar the supple, unblemished kneecaps she observed just beneath the hem of her dress in the photo. Neither she nor her husband was so naïve to think they were invincible. They both had come of age during the eras of Jim Crow and the Civil Rights movement after all. So, they knew better. But, having weathered the storms of the assassinations of both Kennedy and King, the latter occurring on her birthday no less, a part of her surely hoped they had filled their quota of real tragedy for a lifetime. The confident, erect postures and beaming smiles she observes in the photo, not to mention their "nothing can stop us now" demeanors, were perfectly understandable. It was so much easier to be hopeful then, as they contemplated what they could make of their lives together, with so much more of it ahead of them than behind them. Or so they thought.

Pain in the lower region of her back that jolted her awake hours earlier better than any alarm clock returns for an afternoon visit, compelling her left hand's journey to her lower vertebrae.

"Hello, friend," she mutters. "Just couldn't stay away, could you?"

She considers whether to move to the chair on the opposite side of the room to activate the back massage equipment her son had purchased for her last Christmas, but opts not to. She instead makes a fist, kneads and rubs in an effort to hasten her return visitor's exit.

"Now, don't you have something better to do today than come around and bug me?" she asks.

As if being coaxed by an award-winning director, the tension eventually exits stage left, prompting the woman's much-needed sigh of relief.

"Whew!" the woman exclaims. She removes her hand from her back. "Finally."

She scoops the photo of her pet off the table, kisses it, then lowers it to the ottoman. Her eyes move from the photo of her dog to the black framed photo of her son. It sits next to the one of her younger self, her younger self's Afro and her husband. She smiles. The pride she feels in what her first born has accomplished during his more than half century on the planet compels a smile. But short-lived are these thoughts. They begin to sour as she considers the real possibility that tragedy from any number of sources could befall him, just as it did her husband. She commences a quick mental calculation. Five more years before her son reaches the same age at which her husband transitioned from this life to the next. Does a similar fate await her son? She frowns. She repeats the familiar refrain she mastered minutes earlier.

"No, uh-uh. Can't do this."

She shakes her head. She redirects her gaze from the photo of her son until it reaches that of her daughter, whose picture is encased within a silver frame on the other side of the one of her, her Afro puff and her husband. She smiles. Pride swells. The strength within the woman her daughter has become amazes her, not to mention the apparent ease with which she masters motherhood, career and wifery. But she is mindful of the reality—how difficult and stressful it can be. She lived it. That's why she relishes each call from her daughter, especially those accompanied by requests for a visit to "help with the girls." Her granddaughters, both of whom blossom with thoughts, opinions and personalities of their own can be quite a handful. They are also, quite simply, her lifeline.

Menacing thoughts begin to compete for attention with those of her daughter and granddaughters. Images of the NBA star whose life was taken at the tender age of forty-one, alongside that of his daughter and seven others, flash before her. Tragedy consumed his family in an instant when his helicopter crashed seemingly out of nowhere. Her daughter is on the cusp of reaching her forty-first year. What if...?

The familiar school bell ring tone abruptly and loudly invades the woman's airspace, rescuing her from her melancholy malaise. She reaches for her smartphone. Instinct compels her to swipe the bottom of her screen to activate the device without checking the caller ID. She speaks.

"Hello?"

"Hey, Nana!"

"Well, hey there!" the woman replies. She smiles, wipes the vestiges of moisture from her cheek.

"Mommy wants to talk to you," her nine-year-old granddaughter says.

"Okay," the woman replies.

"Hey, Mom," her daughter says.

"Hi," the woman replies. "How are you?"

"Oh, we're fine," her daughter says. "I'm getting the girls ready for church and thought I'd give you a call to see how you're doing."

"It's a rough one today, babe," the woman replies. "I'm not gon' lie."

"I know it is," her daughter says. "The girls and I just want you to know we're thinking about you and praying for you."

"Hang in there, Nana!" her older granddaughter's voice exclaims faintly from the background. "We love you!"

"Well, thank you," the woman replies. "I love you too."

"She just left the room."

"I'm not surprised," the woman replies, laughing. "Busy as ever and cannot sit still."

"You know your granddaughter."

"And the other?" the woman asks. "What is she up to this morning?"

"She's right here in my lap taking a bottle. Eyes barely open and fighting sleep, as usual," her daughter replies. "I'm hoping she'll take a quick nap before we head out."

"Well, good luck with that," the woman says.

"Thanks," her daughter replies.

"So, the other reason I'm calling is that I need to head to Europe for work in about three weeks. I wanted to see if you could come up to help Jacob with the girls while I'm away. He sure could use it. If you've got something planned, I totally understand, but—"

"Oh, no," the woman says. "I can drive up. Just let me know what the dates are when you get a chance."

"Will do," her daughter replies. Sobs from the younger granddaughter begin to escalate in volume.

"Bottle must be empty," the woman says.

"You got it," her daughter replies.

"I knew it," the woman says.

"I'll text you," her daughter replies.

"Okay, sounds good," the woman says.

The faint sound of her older granddaughter's voice again finds its way to the woman's phone.

"Mommy, don't hang up yet!" she exclaims. "I need to talk to Nana."

"Okay, here," the woman's daughter says. She passes the phone.

"Hey, Nana. Don't hang up yet!"

"Yes," the woman replies. "I'm still here."

"Okay, so," her granddaughter begins. "At school we're going to start having these theme days once a week where we have to dress up to match the theme and Mommy showed me some pictures of you when you were, like, younger."

"Uh-huh," the woman replies.

"Okay, so," her older granddaughter continues. "I like that picture Mommy showed me of you with my granddad when your hair was, like, poofy and stuff."

"The one with me and my Afro?" the woman asks.

"Um, yeah, your Afro," her older granddaughter replies. "Well, Mommy said that picture was taken in the seventies. Is that right?"

"Sure is," the woman replies. "Before your Mommy was even born."

"Oh, cool! Well, the next time you come, can you show me how to get my hair like that?" her granddaughter asks. "I wanna wear it like that when we have our '70s-theme day."

"I sure will," the woman replies.

"Yea!" her older granddaughter exclaims. "Thanks, Nana. I love you. And don't cry too much today."

"I won't cry too much, baby," the woman replies. "I love you too!"

"Okay, bye!" her older granddaughter exclaims.

"Bye, baby," the woman replies.

The woman glances over at the photo with her and her husband. She smiles briefly. She unfolds and lifts her body from the recliner and begins to walk toward her bedroom.

"Hmmm, what to wear, what to wear," she mutters to herself. "Something that will look good with my polka dot scarf perhaps."